PENGUIN

Armed with

'We need Mary Butts now, to g... through mazes and forests to the pure sources of storytelling' John Ashbery

'A sophisticated and most exquisitely written fantasy ... There is no doubt that Miss Butts is a poet and writer of often distinguished prose. And once you enter her world ... what goes on becomes exciting and unpredictable, Aldous Huxley and William Blake walking hand in hand, with what results one can perhaps imagine' *The New York Times*

'What she had ... was a new to literature sense of the psychological nuance of emotions exaggerated or created by the war ... She was exploring the new type of emotion for which we have not yet words' Bryher (Winifred Ellerman)

'*Armed with Madness* will assume its rightful place within the canon of Modernist prose' Lawrence Rainey, *London Review of Books*

'Butts joins my pantheon of great eccentric writers such as Jane Bowles, Ivy Compton-Burnett, Henry Green and Denton Welch ... Reading her you feel on the verge of waking from an unrelatable dream' Michael Silverblatt, *LA Style*

'A writer who streaked brightly, like a shooting star, across the firmament of international modernism' Oliver Conant, *New York Times Book Review*

ABOUT THE AUTHOR

Mary Butts was born in 1890 in Dorset where she spent her childhood.
She studied Latin and Greek at Westfield College, London, and social
work at the London School of Economics. During the First World
War she worked for the London County Council and then the
National Council for Civil Liberties. In 1918 she married John
Rodker, a poet, publisher and conscientious objector, with whom she
had a daughter, Camilla. She began publishing poems and stories in
important literary reviews of the time, including *The Little Review*, *The
Dial* and *The Egoist*. She spent most of the 1920s in France, moving in
literary and artistic circles in the company, among others, of Gertrude
Stein, H. D. (Hilda Doolittle), William Carlos Williams, and Ford
Madox Ford. Her most important literary friendship was with Jean
Cocteau who provided drawings for editions of two of her works. *Speed
the Plough and Other Stories* appeared in 1923 and *Ashe of Rings*, her first
novel, in 1925. Her second novel, *Armed with Madness*, was published in
1928, as was the novella *Imaginary Letters*.

In 1930 she returned to England, finally settling in Cornwall with her
second husband, Gabriel Aitken. She published two historical novels,
The Macedonian (1933) and *Scenes from the Life of Cleopatra* (1935), as well
as a further volume of stories. She also reviewed extensively for a
number of magazines and papers. Mary Butts died in 1937. Her auto-
biography, *The Crystal Cabinet*, was published posthumously that same
year.

Although a figure on the literary scene and in contact with many of the
important writers of the time, Butts remained marginal: her interests
and writing put her out of line with any group or movement. Largely
forgotten after her death, her work is now being rediscovered and her
particular contribution as a modernist writer reassessed.

Stephen Heath is a Fellow of Jesus College, Cambridge.

MARY BUTTS

Armed with Madness

With an Introduction by Stephen Heath

PENGUIN BOOKS

PENGUIN BOOKS

Published by the Penguin Group
Penguin Books Ltd, 27 Wrights Lane, London W8 5TZ, England
Penguin Putnam Inc., 375 Hudson Street, New York, New York 10014, USA
Penguin Books Australia Ltd, Ringwood, Victoria, Australia
Penguin Books Canada Ltd, 10 Alcorn Avenue, Toronto, Ontario, Canada M4V 3B2
Penguin Books India (P) Ltd, 11, Community Centre, Panchsheel Park, New Delhi – 110 017, India
Penguin Books (NZ) Ltd, Private Bag 102902, NSMC, Auckland, New Zealand
Penguin Books (South Africa) (Pty) Ltd, 5 Watkins Street, Denver Ext 4, Johannesburg 2094, South Africa

Penguin Books Ltd, Registered Offices: Harmondsworth, Middlesex, England

First published in Great Britain by Wishart and in the USA by Boni 1928
This edition of the text published, with *Death of Felicity Taverner*, in the USA by McPherson & Company 1992
Published in Great Britain with a new Introduction, in Penguin Classics 2001
1

Contents

Introduction: Chances of the Sacred Game

"The effect of Mary Butts' unretouched negatives of raw nerves is quietly, darkly affecting," wrote the American poet Marianne Moore in 1933, seeking to convey her appreciation of a writer whose novels stood somewhat apart in the 1920s and 1930s; as they still do, not easily available and largely unread. *Ashe of Rings* (1925), *Armed With Madness* (1928) and *Death of Felicity Taverner* (1932), all of them set mainly in the Dorset countryside Butts so passionately cherished, offered a style and a vision that met the concerns of her age with a disturbingly particular voice. Of the three, *Armed With Madness* is doubtless the most interesting and original achievement, not least because it is less firmly contained than the others, less driven by a set of ideas that the development of the narrative then confirms. Rather, it takes us immediately and disconcertingly into an edgy world where "nothing [goes on] happening" and "noises let through silence", where the sheer style of the writing holds moments of illumination, flashes of beauty, which at the same time reveal an underlying disquiet. "There is trouble about. The kind that comes with brightness," says Ross to Scylla early in the novel: "Can you see that?" That indeed is what Scylla and the reader will see, as the novel catches them up in a game which brings with it a great deal that is raw and dark. Butts often quoted a line from an Elizabethan poem by Thomas Nashe, written "In Time of Pestilence": "Brightness falls from the air." Her world too is one of sickness, of "dis-ease" (the term used by her and her characters): brightness is falling, meanings are uncertain, and the moments of illumination "always take a turn for the worse".

*

Butts was born in Parkstone in Dorset in 1890 to a retired army officer and his much younger wife. The family house, Salterns, and the countryside surrounding it gave her childhood a magical sense of place to which her writings return. Thanks to her father and the Butts lineage, in which she took much pride, her childhood was also "saturated with the arts", as she put it in her autobiographical memoir, *The Crystal Cabinet* (1937). Her great-grandfather, Thomas Butts, had been a patron and friend of William Blake, whose pictures filled a room of the house (the title of her memoir is from a poem by Blake). The death of her father when she was fourteen (as if "a strong, small, gold sun had set") left her and her four-year-old brother Tony in the hands of their mother, towards whom Butts felt little more than hatred, regarding her as the representative of a middle-class philistinism, incapable of anything other than a commercial response to the land and the art that Mary loved (her mother sold both Salterns and the Blakes). She was sent to finish her education at a school in St Andrews in Scotland and from there went on to Westfield College, London. At Westfield, she studied Latin and Greek, rebelled against conventions, wrote Sapphic poetry and was described by the Principal as a "mad idiot" (the Dostoievskian ring of that would have pleased her). Required to leave when it was discovered that she and a Westfield mistress for whom she had a passion had gone off to the Derby together, she enrolled in social studies courses at the London School of Economics and at the start of the war began working in the East End for the London County Council and then for the National Council of Civil Liberties, particularly concerned at the time with the rights of conscientious objectors. In the last years of the war she was torn between two lovers: Eleanor Rogers, with whom she lived and about whom little is known, and John Rodker, a poet and publisher, imprisoned as a conscientious objector, whom she married in 1918. The couple had a daughter, Camilla, who was left in the care of others, and Butts, who died when her daughter was sixteen, rarely saw her ("motherhood was not Mary Butts's forte", as Camilla was to comment). In 1920 she left Rodker for Cecil Maitland, a writer badly affected by his war experiences, and lived with him, mainly in Paris, until their separation in 1925. In France, and indeed throughout her adult life, which was lived to the full with a restless bohemian lawlessness, Butts was a heavy consumer of alcohol, cocaine, heroin, opium and anything else available (in her final years in Cornwall she brewed up poppy heads and knocked back generous quantities of "Champagne Wine Nerve Tonic", a potent stimulant discovered in a local shop). What relations she had with her mother were bitter, turning largely on matters of money and the Butts inheritance, and those with her brother became equally strained (Tony in 1932 was assuring Virginia Woolf that Mary was a pretentious bad woman: a corrupter of young men who "are always committing suicide").

Already in London Butts had published poetry and fiction in some of the significant literary reviews of the time (*The Little Review*, for example, with the support of Ezra Pound). In the Paris of the 1920s she found herself one of a host of English, Irish and American expatriate writers, meeting Gertrude Stein, James Joyce, H.D., Djuna Barnes, Ford Madox Ford and William Carlos Williams, among many others. She also spent periods in Villefranche-sur-Mer, near Nice, where she became close to Jean Cocteau, who was regularly to be found there with his entourage of young men (the "Achilles set", as Butts called them). It was in Villefranche too that she met and fell in love with the bisexual painter Gabriel Aitken, marrying him in 1930. During this time her writing continued: *Speed the Plough and Other Stories* was published in 1923 and her first novel, *Ashe of Rings*, in 1925. Two books followed in 1928: *Armed With Madness* and *Imaginary Letters*, the latter a novella, set in Paris, dealing with a woman's love for a homosexual Russian émigré and drawing directly, as does so much of Butts's work, on biographical material. At the beginning of the 1930s she and Aitken moved back to England, finally settling in Sennen Cove on the Cornish coast, where Butts lived for the rest of her life; alone from 1935, when Aitken left her after a series of homosexual affairs. During these Cornish years, she published *Death of Felicity Taverner* (1932), a novel that picks up characters and setting from *Armed With Madness*, followed by two historical novels, *The Macedonian* (1933) and *Scenes from the Life of Cleopatra* (1935). The latter, together with the many reviews and short articles she contributed to newspapers and magazines, gave her a somewhat wider readership. There was a further collection of stories, *Several Occasions* (1932), and two pamphlets on the ills of contemporary civilization, *Traps for Unbelievers* and *Warning to Hikers* (both 1932). A final collection of stories was published after her death in 1937 as *Last Stories* (1938). Her books were subsequently allowed to go out of print and she disappeared from attention, barely mentioned, if at all, in literary histories, though her work was read by certain writers in the United States (notably by poets: Frank O'Hara, John Ashbery, Robert Duncan and Jack Spicer among others).

Looking back on her life, Butts regarded it as "a series of initiations". What is clear is that it embraced a number of positions, with shifts and turns that, while often contradictory in the directions taken, are always sustained by a strong reaction to the age and its discontents and a concern to grasp and urge some other, vital truth of things—the "initiations" are the cardinal experiences that put her in contact with this truth. Her childhood, as she recounts it, was filled with revelations of "the mystery of being", culminating in an intense experience at Badbury Rings, the Iron Age earthworks near Wimborne Minster, where she felt herself to have been magically "received", "accepted", brought to a deep awareness of "power, movement, a pattern" (the words are those of the heroine of *Ashe of Rings*, a novel in which Butts relies heavily on the Rings experience). Her young womanhood saw her rebellious, sexually adventurous, pacifist, feminist in certain of her views (though she disliked feminism and was no part of any women's movement) and a self-declared socialist (again, this is a matter of certain attitudes rather than of sustained political commitment). She was a socialist, however, for whom what was essential lay beyond social reality and who was intent on phenomena she felt to be inexplicable by known physical laws; hence her study of magic and the occult (the study included a few primitive months in Sicily with the self-proclaimed magus Aleister Crowley at his "Abbey of Thelema", taking "astral journeys" to new planes of consciousness; Crowley, for whom women were "dangerous to the career of a magician", was irritated and unnerved by the independent-minded, wilful Butts, whose involvement with magic never destroyed her streak of tough common sense). Though she moved in modernist literary and artistic circles, she also remained marginal, not easily to be identified with any group or movement, and this not least because of her overriding sense of "an immediate supernatural", her belief in some spiritual or magical or mystical "thing" that it was the purpose of her writing to approach. She had contacts with Bloomsbury, for example, but remained unassimilable, out of step with its ways of thinking which she could regard only as a sterile attempt to find reductive explanations for forces beyond the grasp of the intellect (reciprocally, Bloomsbury in the person of Virginia Woolf had little time for "the malignant Mary"). Indicatively, Butts herself seems typically to have been drawn to individuals or groups in one way or another excluded or exiled: her attraction to homosexual men is one instance; that to White Russians who had fled the Revolution another (Boris in *Armed With Madness* combines both). In Cornwall, after "years of disbelief ... every fashionable kind of scepticism, magic, etc.", she declared her socialism to have been an error of childhood, issued her pamphlets for the times, and espoused Anglo-Catholicism.

*

Armed With Madness was written between the end of 1925 and the middle of 1927, much of it during periods spent in Villefranche. It was published in London in June of the following year by Wishart & Company, a new publishing house committed to taking literary works regarded as not commercially attractive by other publishers; in addition to the trade edition, Wishart brought out a special edition of a hundred copies with three drawings by Cocteau (an entry in Virginia Woolf's diary of August 1927 suggests that she earlier rejected the novel for publication by the Hogarth Press). It received a fair number of reviews, many of them acknowledging its distinctiveness while regretting what was regarded as its difficulty, indeed by some as *its* madness. Even one of her most loyal supporters, Hugh Ross Williamson, the editor of *The Bookman*, which published numerous pieces by her, was later to regret that "when in 1928, Mary Butts made her bow to the English public with a novel, it was unfortunately with a work so difficult to understand that it was almost a despair to her admirers"; he acknowledged, however, that it was the epitome of her writing. Marianne Moore stressed the novel's distinctiveness as Butts's triumph: "it is a mistake to recount anything she writes without recounting it in her own words."

In 1925 Butts had read Arthur Waite's *The Holy Grail* (1909), a lengthy account of "the deeper suggestions of the Grail legends", and sketched out an idea for a play turning on the discovery of an object taken as the Grail. By early 1926 she was thinking of a country-house novel to "begin with 'boys and girls' finding the Grail cup. At S. Egliston"; or again, as she noted when completing the book: "erroneous find of the importance of the Sanc-grail—reactions in a country home, the Foyot and the Bœuf sur le Toit" (the Foyot is a Parisian hotel, the Bœuf a celebrated Parisian nightclub of the twenties where, in the words of a contemporary observer, "just about everyone but Proust was to be seen"). Probably, Butts was remembering a newspaper story of 1907, mentioned in writings on the Holy

Grail by Arthur Machen, concerning the supposed find of the Grail cup—"a saucer-shaped vessel of blue glass, shot with silver"—in a well or stream near Glastonbury (the man who placed the cup there got it from his father, another suggestion from the story which finds its way into *Armed With Madness*).

The country-house, the "boys and girls", the "erroneous find", the Grail—these are central to the novel. The house is, naturally, in Dorset, isolated, near the coast, enclosed by a wood, with two paths running down through it to the sea. Butts had in mind the situation of the house in South Egliston in which she stayed in 1922: "a cottage at the top of the sacred wood under Tyneham cap". This is Butts's country, her *place*: precisely experienced, magically imagined, sacred. The inhabitants of the house are a sister and brother, Scylla and Felix Taverner, an "ash-fair tree-tall young woman" who wants to let things unfold to their utmost possibility, and "a flower-skinned, sapphire-eyed boy", given to anger and self-pity and fed up with "the baby-brother business"; and a friend, Ross, possessed of a sacred peace, content with the simple satisfaction of his appetites; and two more friends, Clarence and Picus, who come over from their nearby cottage when their well dries up—the former war-scarred and suffering from the age's lack of faith, the latter a cousin of Scylla's, "light and winged and holy" but bringing tricks and trouble and pain.* The time is the 1920s, not long after the Great War

* Picus is a complex mythological figure, possessed of prophetic powers and usually taking the form of a woodpecker, the sacred bird of Mars. It is with Picus as woodpecker linked with Zeus, the great thunder-hurling god of Greek mythology, that *Armed With Madness* is concerned. Butts was familiar with the discussion of "the woodpecker-king" and "bird-magic" in the classical scholar Jane Harrison's *Themis: A Study of the Social Origins of Greek Religion* (1912). Harrison stresses the identification of the woodpecker with Zeus and provides Butts with the line quoted by Scylla from the *Suda*, a Greek literary encyclopedia compiled at the end of the tenth century AD: "Here lies the Woodpecker who is also Zeus." For Harrison, "Picus enshrines a beautiful lost faith,

which hangs over the novel; Scylla is of the generation before it; Felix is younger and missed it; Clarence and Picus served in it. All the characters are distant from any specific social life; none works; the men are artistic (Ross and Clarence are accomplished painters, Picus makes wax models of Scylla, Felix manages still lives of poisonous-looking flowers). A few secondary figures make appearances or are heard of—the Taverners' old nanny, a fisherman, a drunk and obscene shepherd and his wife, the local doctor—but are barely more than novelistic class stereotypes. There is a gramophone and the latest records but not much more of the period specifically enters. Far from the imperatives of a social realism, Butts's novel is itself enclosed in different concerns, in a different writing.

The novels begins with an arrival, that of the American, Carston, disturbing the peace. What follows is the playing out of a drama in which characters tensely interact until a breaking-point is reached at which they disperse, going their different ways before the novel reassembles them for a violent moment of madness and an ending that brings no resolution, only another arrival, another foreign body; this time a White Russian with no papers, brought over from France in a boat by Felix and landing with him at the foot

---

the faith that birds and beasts had *mana* other and sometimes stronger than the *mana* of man." (*Mana*, which also occurs in *Armed With Madness*, is a Melanesian term which refers to an invisible power or vital energy which permeates the world; certain animals or places or people being particularly charged with *mana* and so as particularly sacred; *tabu* recognizes *mana* as a dangerous force and the attitude of scruple or avoidance.) Butts too doubtless knew, or knew of, *Picus Who is Also Zeus* (1916) by Rendel Harris, which explains the identification from the primitive belief that the thunder was a bird: the Great Black Woodpecker, *Picus Martius*. Hence the numerous references to Butts's Picus as bird-like and specifically as "the woodpecker"; hence too his dual reality—just a character in the novel like any other but also unlike, imbued with an uncanny difference, a mythical significance; he sets off the sacred game through his trick with the cup, leads Scylla into the secret wood, has something of the magician in his manipulation of *mana*.

of their cliff just as Carston is leaving for ever, glad to get away from this "stable and unstable" household. Clarence and Picus bring news of a find: "an odd cup of greenish stone" fished up from the bottom of their well. The cup is just an object, a piece of jade that can be used as an ash-tray, but queer too, a recipient for different identifications: variously declared to be "a victorian finger-bowl", "the poison-cup of a small rajah", "an old cup of the sacrament people called 'big magic'", or "a Keltic mass cup". "I can't tell you anything," says the wise Vicar consulted as to its identity, who counsels that it be taken back to the well, keeping its silence; "Why couldn't the thing speak," Carston frets, "Just once. Dumb was the word for it." In the movement of the novel, however, the cup is not dumb. It provokes incidents, sets off characters, runs into meanings, *reveals*. This at one level is quite conventional: the cup is a bit of property owned by Picus's father that Picus has taken and dropped down the well; perhaps accidentally, more probably with the intention of playing a trick. The cup plunges the novel into Picus's particular family romance: his love of his mother and his hostility towards his father, whom he believes, or wants to believe, poisoned her with the help of his mistress, "his whore"—a whole Freudian scenario. It also involves the other characters in psychological conflict as they react to the find and then to the cup's disappearance (Picus hides it); Carston in particular who, at a loss for a role (the constant emphasis is on the staging of a drama), decides that his purpose will be to seduce Scylla but then finds himself caught up in a very different action, a very different novel. For at another level, and most importantly, the cup is more than a psychological prop, a catalyst to bring out private griefs and sexual pains. With it comes the Grail story on which the imagination of the novel turns and with which it seeks to give its vision of dis-ease.

Soon after completing *Armed With Madness*, Butts noted that it might have been called *The Waste Land* and that she and

T. S. Eliot were "working on a parallel" with the Grail story; save that he was working on its negative—waste land—side, while she was trying to push towards its positive one (the affinities between Butts and Eliot, "the american poet" from whom she quotes in *Armed With Madness*, were real—significantly, both were led to Anglo-Catholicism—but Butts had nothing of Eliot's Calvinist heritage and Puritanical temperament; though they intersect at points, their lives and writing are very different). Eliot was to claim regret at having sent readers off "on a wild goose chase after Tarot cards and the Holy Grail". For Butts, such an attitude would have been impossible: the Grail is no wild goose chase and her use of the story is bound up with her conviction of its fundamental truth, making it a necessary reference for her in a novel dealing with the chaos of the modern world—the Grail story is *essential*. For all the trickery and all the Freudian bits and pieces surrounding it, the cup in *Armed With Madness* allows a spiritual adventure, engages the characters in the sacred game. "We live fast," says Scylla, "and are always having adventures, adventures which are like patterns of another adventure going on somewhere else all the time." The material fact of the cup is as nothing to the strength of the experience it provokes, the possibility it gives of awareness of that other adventure. "This story as I see it is true Sanc-Grail," says the old man present at the consultation with the Vicar and continues with what is effectively a summary of *Armed With Madness* itself: "it seems to me that you are having something like a ritual. A find, illumination, doubt and division, collective and then dispersed." The idea of ritual is fundamental. For Butts, myths, rites, sacraments, all stem from "universal natural events" and bear on "the health and ill-health of the soul". This is what the sacred game is about, a game in which we take chances, risk what truth we may discover. Butts was highly critical of Aldous Huxley for his atheism but enthusiastic about *Antic Hay* (1923) which she thought unique among his novels for its "implicit design, as though there lay behind it, maimed and exceedingly strange, a ritual dance as old as time or man". Whether or not that is a good description of *Antic Hay*, it says much of the intended design and effect of *Armed With Madness*.

"There was something wrong with all of them, or with their world." Butts's diagnosis of the ill-health of the age is uncompromising: the modern world is in denial of essential, spiritual truth. *Traps for Unbelievers* was her account of what she saw as the bankruptcy of religion and the consequences of the disappearance of "the whole complex of emotions we call the religious attitude." This is the critical condition indicated by Butts through Scylla's reflections at the start of *Armed With Madness*: "But everywhere there was a sense of broken continuity, a dis-ease. The end of an age, the beginning of another. Revaluation of values. Phrases that meant something if you could mean them." The war is a major factor in this sense of broken continuity; as is the alienation from the land of the mass of the population in an urban, industrial society; as is capitalism with its creation of a middle-class culture devoid of any but directly material values. The doctor's mention of Wagner's *Parsifal* (1882) when the characters play "the Freud game" of giving associations prompted by the cup is important here. Though Butts disliked much in Wagner's treatment of the Grail story, she responded powerfully to the music and perfectly understood his urge to grasp in the mythical images of religion "the concealed deep truth within them" (as he put it in *Religion and Art*, 1880). Significantly, Wagner could think of the Grail as in contrast to the gold of the *Ring*, which is deprived of its "ideal content" by Alberich's theft and the forging of the ring, this reducing it to a "real content" as possession, coveted for the power it gives; the Grail is anti-capital, not material wealth but revelation of *divine* riches. In *Armed With Madness*, Picus's father expounds his rights of ownership and can see the cup only as "Prupperty: prupperty: prupperty"; everything that Butts values is swept aside as mere superstition, which is to say "A disgusting relic of non-understood natural law."

It is against such reductionism that Butts stands. As Scylla tells Carston: "If the materialist's universe is true, not a working truth to make bridges with and things, we are a set of blind factors in a machine. And no passion has any validity and no imagination. They are just little tricks of the machine. It either is so, or it isn't. If you hold that it isn't, you corrupt your intellect by denying certain facts. If you stick to the facts as we have them, life is a horror and an insult." There is no question for Butts of an overall refusal of materialist scientific explanations, no denying certain facts, but no question either of allowing such explanations the custody of the truth of the imagination, the emotions, religious experience. She was interested in the new physics, not least for its own challenge to orthodox materialist assumptions, but found nothing in that or the new psychology ("the merry-go-round of the complex and the wish-fulfilment and the conditioned reflex") that could replace the beliefs shattered by the discoveries of science. Religion, and with religion the health of humankind, depends on recognition of a spiritual whole, the wholeness of a natural world transfused by the supernatural. Like many writers of the time, and in parallel again with Eliot, she was influenced by Sir James Frazer's massive proto-anthropological study *The Golden Bough* (1890–1915), finding in its wide-ranging discussion of myths and rituals much to discover about magical and religious forms and valuing it for what Eliot described as the light it threw "on the obscurities of the soul". Frazer's account of his material, however, was one of an evolutionary movement from magic and religion to science; his underlying rationalist purpose was to challenge superstition. "What narrowness of spiritual life we find in Frazer," commented Wittgenstein in 1931, reacting against the treatment of magical and religious notions as though they were so many mistakes, so much "false physics": "his explanations of the primitive observances are much cruder than the sense of the observances themselves". Butts would have agreed.

Much of Butts's critique of the modern world is conventional, readily understandable within the radical conservative tradition of the criticism of "civilization" developed throughout the nineteenth century and continued in the first decades of the twentieth (the tradition described in Raymond Williams's *Culture and Society*); for all the differences, *Traps for Unbelievers* and *Warning to Hikers* can reasonably be read alongside, say, Eliot's *After Strange Gods* (1934) and *The Idea of a Christian Society* (1939). The particular inflection of Butts's critique comes from her magical sense of place, the significance she gives to "the land" which she sees as being rapidly destroyed. This destruction, in *Armed With Madness*, as in *Warning to Hikers* and so much of her writing, is represented by "tourists". Starn, the nearest village in the novel, is remembered by Carston as "half full of people from the world outside. Not peasants, people in vulgar clothes, on motorcycles, in Ford cars, come to stare because it was summer, whom his party treated as if they were a disease." Tourists here are taken as an evident symptom of the process of desecration that railways and cars and new forms of leisure activity bring with them. On the one hand, Butts is insistent on the vital need for contact with the land (if city-dwellers "do not get back to some kind of contact with the earth, civilization will perish out of England"); on the other, contemporary attempts to regain contact are simply a violation (people bringing "their city vulgarities into the serenest and loveliest places"). *Warning to Hikers* gives strident expression to this double bind, mixing bits of Ruskin, Nietzsche and others into a general indictment of industrial capitalism and democracy ("the enemy is the democratic enemy") with a specific focus on the contemporary "cult of nature". Industrial manufacture produces "unvarying patterns of ugly vulgarity", with the result that "a whole people has lost its power to distinguish between what is ugly and what is beautiful"; people are separated from the essential power of nature, which they then try to recover but are able only to do so in ways that confirm their alienation from it. Hikers—this was the great moment of the development of rambling—bring with them the very ugliness from which they seek to escape, incapable as they have been made of truly grasping nature's mystery: "Either they destroy what they find or are lost in it ... Lost and mindless and in fear." In *Death of Felicity Taverner*, the novel which follows *Armed With Madness*, with the same Dorset setting and some of the same characters, the evil Kralin is bent on exploiting this false return to the country by buying up the Taverners' sacred wood and the surrounding land in order to develop a leisure complex, with hotels, golf courses, car parks and "a cinema ... with all the new sex films".

Kralin is another kind of foreign body, to be rejected, eliminated (and so at the end of the novel Boris, one of the characters carried over from *Armed With Madness*, duly kills him). His father fled the pre-Revolution Russia of the Tsars, not, like Boris, that of the Bolsheviks; the son is nihilistically materialist, probably a Red agent: a "superficial, scientific pornographist", indifferent to moral values and recognizing no truth other than that there is no truth. He is also Jewish; except that "also" is misleading, since it is Jewishness that underpins this nihilism, that defines him as threatening. Though, significantly—a further twist—he is not even a "proper Jew" of devout religious and moral observance; but then of course, in this version of things, the distinction between proper and improper is a construction of the anti-semitism itself, which then trades too on the possibility the fantasy construction provides of collapsing the distinction—all Jews are potentially Kralins. Butts is close here to the Eliot of the notorious comment made the year after publication of *Death of Felicity Taverner* that "reasons of race and religion combine to make any large number of free-thinking Jews undesirable". Kralin, "a man whose interests were all cerebral", represents in this novel the negation at the heart of the modern world and, more particularly, the end of all hope of the "proper balance between urban and rural" for which Eliot called immediately after his "undesirable" comment. Butts's anti-semitism here is not simply a personal fact—to be explained, say, by animosity towards Rodker, her Jewish first husband. It is part of a cultural structure to which *Death of Felicity Taverner* gives rank expression and in which Jews stand as agents and symptoms of a felt decline of social cohesion and stable values.

There is a small trace of this in *Armed With Madness* when Philip, the husband of Scylla's friend in London, is reported in his wife's thoughts as having "gone out to meet a Jew whose favour they were nursing"; nursing no doubt in the interests of a deal of some kind. Philip, stupidly middle class, smug in his petty moralism, is aggressively hostile to the Taverners and their lifestyle and "The Jew" appears, as it were, as the edge of that hostility, adding briefly to Butts's presentation of the forces antagonistic to her values, though here the formulation belongs to the wife and may be read as contained within the terms of the presentation *of her*. More generally, however, those values as expressed in the conception of the sacred land and given through the Grail story can easily come to seem to have precisely as a condition of their existence some negative outside force against which they can be defended, against which sanctity can be defined. In *Armed With Madness* we have the vulgar tourist masses and the philistine middle classes (figured by Philip and by Picus's father); in *Death of Felicity Taverner*, the nihilistic Jew, as Butts collapses social into racial criticism and the novel becomes flatly conventional in its plot, its ideas, its anti-semitism (this from a writer capable in a review of Nancy Cunard's *Negro Anthology* of writing with some thought on "race-prejudice").

The strength of *Armed With Madness* is its uncertainty. There is little plot, no neat ending, no ideologically forced resolution. Its enclosed country-house drama of dis-ease, that the Grail story underlies and informs with a sense of what has been lost, peters out in griefs and wounds and doubts and fragmentations. The adventure can be seen as a "parody of a mystery", getting nowhere since there is nowhere to be got ("'Then we get nowhere.' 'Nowhere'"); it is "complicated, violent, inconclusive". The dispersal of the characters after the first Dorset part of the novel is an indication of this. The novel abandons the sequence of numbered chapters and breaks off into a series of short sections with separate headings that shift disconnectedly from character to character (this can be seen, less sharply, earlier in the novel, which, in modernist style, shifts between different centres of consciousness, but there within the narration of a common story). Scylla in London confronts the pettiness of social conventions; Felix home-sick in Paris carries his inferiority complex from bar to bar; Picus prostrates himself weeping on his mother's grave; Clarence cannot find escape from madness; Ross paints. The return of the novel's focus to Dorset continues the disintegration, violently expressed in Clarence's crazed assault on Scylla. As Carston leaves, Felix appears with Boris, the new find, and the novel ends, inconclusively indeed, on a memory from the latter's childhood, a fragment of a past as though tacked on, another country-house, another wood, the nostalgia of loss.

"The worst is coming to the worst with our civilization"; but also, "something ... is trying to get born ... a 'spiritual' or 'magical', a mystical thing." Knowledge of the waste land is already awareness of something beyond. This is the positive emphasis against, as Butts sees it, Eliot's negative one in *The Waste Land*. The inconclusiveness of the Grail story itself is important for her in this context: it is the quest—the adventure—that is essential; what counts is awareness, imagination, the quickened sense of "the natural supernatural". The modern problem is the eradication of any such sense, the contemporary blinkering of vision. Butts's project is thus to "show beauty—soundness". The modernist imperative to "make it new" becomes her insistence on the need for a new kind of seeing, of writing away from the given categories. Her problem, therefore, is that of expressing "an unknown in terms of the known": "there aren't any words or shapes, or sounds, or gestures to tell it by—not directly." So it must be told indirectly, obliquely; much as, in Butts's favourite image, the knight in chess moves sideways to go forward. The insertion of the Grail story into her modern novel is itself something of a knight's move: it gets nowhere and yet at the same time allows something to be seen; the present is momentarily translated into another time which is itself lost but there, maimed and strange, an implicit design. This is what gives the peculiar tense of Butts's novel: written in the present but unsettled, over and above the regular—realistic—time of action and characters. She writes and over-writes: always there is a presence of the writing which holds itself up in moments of language, fashions word and image and syntax into flashes on its surface, occasions of brightness. Even the modernist collage technique, which here mixes Celtic legends with spirituals, lines from Eliot or Gershwin with scraps of hermeneutic wisdom, references to Gide or Joyce with snatches from music-hall songs, has its part in this. The writing is scattered with these bits and pieces which enter with no particular directions to the reader (no particular irony resulting from clever juxtapositions, for example). They make their individual sense (this or that quotation will often have some local and perhaps overall significance, most clearly when it relates to magic or the Grail) but are also simply, unemphatically, that which the writing brings along in its elaboration, a cultural-spiritual bric-à-brac that makes up Butts's unstable, unsettled present.

Above all, then, it is her style, her writing, with which Butts *resists*, with which she strives to tell what is only obliquely to be told. Her prose *lets through* colour, silence, uncanniness, something on the other side of the given—the assumed—reality. "Their land, as they knew it, equivocal, exquisite," reflects Scylla, and it is this "equivocal, exquisite" that the style works to render. Immediately, in the opening pages, the wind rises off "the diamond-blue sea", tree-fuchsias drip "with bells the colour of blood", and under everything "the silence in the wood". Wonder and horror come together: the sea sparkles and has the iron-greyness of a gun-barrel; it is "transparent, peacock-coloured" but "under the water the reefs [are] snakes". The blood-belled fuchsias start a trail of blood that winds its way across the novel to end in Scylla's arrow-pierced body, with the blood of the Grail story somewhere under it all. The required awareness brings a wrought preciousness of word, image, syntax, punctuation even: "Half an hour later they had packed into the car and shot away, up into the hills the night wind had now made exquisite, to a different wood from the one in whose red-glass darkness Picus had lost them, moist and shimmering, a repetition of the tremblings of the stars"; "For where the sun was turning down-Channel, a ball glared, surrounded by ranks of rose bars, and out from these clouds radiated that reached over to the eastern heavens, across whose spokes strayed loose flakes dipped in every variety of flame, the triangles of empty sky stained all the greens between primrose and jade"; "a white road sprung like an arrow across the moor that filled the lowlands like a dark dragon's wing."

"Besides," says Picus to Carston in the closing pages, "did you ever enjoy a summer more? Hasn't it been better than a movie?" Ironic enough, coming just after Clarence's frenzy and after all of Carston's frustrations, but true in its way, including in its irony, of the reading of this novel itself. In *Armed With Madness* Butts produced a peculiarly haunting, flawed, strangely original book that, within but aslant the modernist mainstream, forged from period commonplaces and personal intensities a way of seeing, a style, which are immediately recognizable as hers. It deserves to be read along with the other key novels that have come down to us from the 1920s.

Note on the Holy Grail

The legend of the Holy Grail, the cup used by Christ at the Last Supper, was developed in a body of early medieval romances. The cup is associated with St Joseph of Arimathea, who is said to have caught blood in it from the wound in Christ's side made with his spear by the Roman soldier Longinus at the Crucifixion (hence the significance in *Armed With Madness* of the cup having been fished out of the well with a spear). Joseph brought the cup to Britain, where he founded the abbey at Glastonbury which became the Grail shrine. The Grail was lost and became the object of holy quest: to restore purity, the Christian Knight must journey through the desolate world in search of it. The romances vary in their telling of the story but depend in one form or another on: the terrible loss ("what they wanted had been lost out of the world," Scylla tells Carston; adding, "Might have been any time, the Middle Ages, or the day before yesterday"); the strife that befalls the land bereft of the sacred object; and the perilous adventures entailed by the quest. Carston gives a very Buttsian summary for the purposes of *Armed With Madness*: "There had been a story ... of a king, a *comitatus* called Arthur, whose business had been divided between chasing barbarians and looking for a cup. A kind of intermezzo in history, in a time called the Dark Ages, which had produced a story about starlight. Suns of centuries had succeeded it, while the story had lived obscurely in some second-rate literature, and more obscurely, and as an unknown quality, in the imaginations of men like Picus and Scylla, Felix, Clarence and Ross."

The Grail and its legend were a focus of interest in the years preceding and surrounding the writing of *Armed With*

Madness and had been a source for literary and artistic creation (Wagner's *Parsifal* (1882) and Eliot's *The Waste Land* (1922) being outstanding examples of this). In *From Ritual to Romance* (1920) the anthropologist Jessie Weston, inspired by *The Golden Bough*, had argued that the Grail story was "the confused record" of a much earlier ritual, that of a fertility cult: the original ritual has passed into the romance elaboration of the Grail legend, whose main features—for example, the barrenness of the world from which the Grail has vanished—are exactly those of such a cult. The Christianization of the story is purely external to its fundamental meaning, no more than new trappings for the old ritual.

Such an account of the Grail story as the record of a purely pagan legend into which Christian symbolism subsequently intruded was opposed in the period, notably in the work of A. E. Waite and Arthur Machen, both of whom Butts read. Waite, contrary to "the pagan school", emphasized the Christian force of the story and its deep spiritual sense; it deals in "high symbols", presenting "figurations to which the soul confesses on the upward path of its progress". Machen, who saw Waite as wrongly playing down the Celtic elements of the story, was concerned to present it as "the glorified version of early Celtic Sacramental Legend". Machen's insistence on a Celtic origin comes with the idea of an early Christian Church that had its own Eucharistic rite and a closeness to a world beyond this one, experienced magically through numinous places, sacred trees and other such things. "To the Celt, and to those who have the Celtic spirit," wrote Machen, "the whole material universe appears as a vast symbol."

Butts is close to this. Celtic magic and the Celtic church play a large part in her imagination. For her, too, behind the Grail lies another consecration of the Eucharist, a Church which precedes and stands outside the establishment of the Roman Church in Britain that will then oppose it. When Ross in *Armed With Madness* offers as the association with the Grail legend that immediately springs to his mind "A mass said at Corbenic ... a different mass which may have been the real thing", it is precisely to this supposed original Eucharistic rite that he refers, as so often does Butts herself; Corbenic being the castle or church of the Grail where Lancelot witnessed this other mass. Corbenic was, in Machen's words, "scarcely on earth" and the way to it was charted "only on maps of the spirit". It is for its expression of this that the Grail legend is important to Butts. What is at stake for her is "an incident, a not yet exhausted event, in the most secret, passionate and truthful part of the spiritual history of man".

Bibliographical Note

The major resource for knowledge of Butts's life is the recent biography by Nathalie Blondel, *Mary Butts: Scenes from the Life* (Kingston, NY: McPherson & Company, 1998); Blondel was able to draw on, and quote extensively from, the journal kept by Butts for the last twenty years of her life (the Introduction in the present edition is indebted to her work). Important extracts from the journal, together with some Butts letters, can be found in Christopher Wagstaff (ed.), *A Sacred Quest: The Life and Writings of Mary Butts* (Kingston, NY: McPherson & Company, 1995). The *Crystal Cabinet* was republished in 1998 (Manchester: Carcanet, and Boston: Beacon Press). In the last decade or so McPherson & Company has reissued the other novels, a volume of stories and Butts's pamphlets. A volume of stories was also published in Britain in 1991 by Carcanet under the title *With and Without Buttons and Other Stories*. Of the small amount of critical writing on Butts's work, mention should be made of Robin Blaser, "Here Lies the Woodpecker Who was Zeus", in the volume edited by Wagstaff mentioned above, and Patrick Wright's "Coming Back to the Shores of Albion: The Secret England of Mary Butts", in his book *On Living in an Old Country: The National Past in Contemporary Britain* (London: Verso, 1985).

Armed
with
Madness

Armed with madness, I go on a long voyage.

Chapter I

I N THE HOUSE, in which they could not afford to live, it was unpleasantly quiet. Marvellously noisy, but the noises let through silence. The noises were jays, bustling and screeching in the wood, a hay-cutter, clattering and sending up waves of scent, substantial as sea-waves, filling the long rooms as the tide fills a blow-hole, but without roar or release. The third noise was the light wind, rising off the diamond-blue sea. The sea lay three parts round the house, invisible because of the wood. The wood rose from its cliff-point in a single tree, and spread out inland, in a fan to enclose the house. Outside the verandah, a small lawn had been hollowed, from which the wood could be seen as it swept up, hurrying with squirrels, into a group of immense ilex, beech and oak. The lawn was stuck with yuccas and tree-fuchsias, dripping season in, season out, with bells the colour of blood.

Once the house was passed, the wood gave it up, enclosed it decently, fenced a paddock, and the slip of dark life melted into the endless turf-miles which ran up a great down into the sky.

The silence let through by the jays, the hay-cutter, and the breeze, was a complicated production of stone rooms, the natural silence of empty grass, and the equivocal, personal silence of the wood. Not many nerves could stand it. People who had come for a week had been known to leave next day. The people who had the house were interested in the wood and its silence. When it got worse, after dark or at mid-day, they said it was tuning-up. When a gale came up-Channel shrieking like a mad harp, they said they were watching a visible fight with the silence in the wood.

A large gramophone stood with its mouth open on the

verandah flags. They had been playing to the wood after lunch, to appease it and to keep their dancing in hand. The house was empty. Their servants had gone over to a distant farm. The wood had it all its own way. They were out.

There were two paths through the wood to the sea. A bee-line through the high trees, of fine grass, pebble scattered, springing and wet. Then, across the wet ditch that was sometimes a stream, a path through the copse in figures of eight, whose turns startled people. As the wood narrowed, this way ended in a gate on to the grass, the nearest way to an attractive rabbit-warren. These were the only two paths in that country, except a green road which led from the house over the down to the white road and from thence on to the beginnings of the world, ten miles away.

There was only one house except a shepherd's cottage, and a little fancy lodge, the wood had swallowed, which they let to a fisherman in exchange for fish. The fisherman was a gentleman, and a fine carver in wood. The shepherd was a troglodyte. He came home drunk in the moonlight spinning round and yelling obscene words to the tune of old hymns. They were equally friends with both. They belonged to the house and the wood and the turf and the sea; had no money and the instincts of hospitality; wanted everything and nothing, and were at that moment lying out naked on a rock-spit which terminated their piece of land.

The cliffs there were low and soft, rounded with a black snout, but based on a wedge of orange stone, smooth and running out square under the sea.

Up and down the channel, high cliffs rose, airy, glittering, but some way off. Their headland was low, their valley shallow and open, spiked only with undersea reefs, no less lovely and disastrous than the famous precipices which made their coast their pride.

"Mare Nostrum," they said, in Paris or in London, at

the sea's winter takings there. An outlet for a natural fe-
rocity they were too proud to exercise, too indifferent to
examine. Also a kind of ritual, a sacrifice, willing but impersonal to their gods.

Meanwhile the weather was good. One of them sat up,
and rolled off the reef's edge into the sea.

A brother and sister to whom the house belonged, and
a young man they had known a long time. They called her
Scylla from her name Drusilla, altering it because they said
she was sometimes a witch and sometimes a bitch. They
were handsome and young, always together, and often
visited by their friends. It was Felix, the brother, who had
swum out. His sister sat up and watched him with the
touch of anxiety common to females, however disciplined.
"Be careful," she called, "the tide's turning." He wallowed
under the sea.

"Leave him alone," said the other man, "it's the last
day's peace," and rolled over on his face and ate pink
sea-weed.

She approved because it was good for his complexion,
wood-brown as they were fair, but she stood up and
watched the boy's head popping in and out of the crisp
water. Naked, the enormous space, the rough earth
dressed her. The sparkling sea did not. But the sea at the
moment was something for the men to swim in, an enormous toy. She thought again: 'He won't drown. Besides,
why worry?' Lay down again, and fed an anemone with a
prawn.

"Ross, why do you say 'the last day's peace'? You like
people when they come."

He answered:

"One always enjoys something. But this one's an
American."

"No, we've never had one before."

"I don't mind 'em. I always like their women. But take
it from me, all we shall get out of this one is some fun. He
won't like the wood. The wood will giggle at him."

"It laughs at us...."

"We don't mind—it's our joke." He laughed, sitting upright staring down-Channel, his head pitched back on an immensely long neck, his mouth like a wild animal's, only objectively pre-occupied with the world. She thought: 'Grin like a dog, and run about the rocks,' accepting him as she accepted everything there. She said: "Give him a good time and see what happens." That was her part of their hospitality, whose rewards were varied and irregular. None of them, with perhaps the exception of Felix, could understand a good time that was not based on flashes of illumination, exercises of the senses, dancing, and stretches of very insular behaviour.

Something long and white came up behind them out of the sea. An extra wave washed Felix a ledge higher. "Thank you," he said and skipped across. "Oh, my dear, I'm sure an octopus caught my leg."

"D'you remember," said Ross, "the chap last winter who killed them with his teeth and fainted at the sight of white of egg?"

The pleasant memory united them; they became a triple figure, like Hecate the witch, amused, imaginative. They put on their things: Felix's pretty clothes, Ross's rough ones, the girl, her delicate strong dress. With their arms round her shoulders, they crossed the rocks and went up the cliff-path, and through the wood to the house.

Chapter II

THEY WOKE to a clean superb day. The high trees broke the sun, and Scylla admired the form of them, standing straight to the east in the natural shape of trees, their tops curled to the west, tightened and distorted against the ocean wind.

Below them the copse was a knit bundle, almost as firm as stone. Still there were long shadows as she dressed, still dance and flash of birds. The wood was innocent, the house fresh and serene. At breakfast, in a quicksilver mirror, she saw the men come in. The eagle over it had a sock-suspender in its beak, but between the straps and the distortion she did not like the look of them.

They meant not to help her with the American, whom they had ordered like a new record from town. Who would have to be met.

They were like that. She was like that herself, but did not manage to give in to it. Which made her despise herself, think herself too female.

All three had work to do. She got hers done, and at the same time believed herself the sole stay of her men. Separated and bound to them because of her service they seemed unable to do without.

Ross was saying, cautiously: "That man's coming today." She wondered what he was thinking about in the train. Staring about and trying to remember the name of the station. A name as familiar as their own. Nothing to him. Fun to make it part of his consciousness? Fun for them. The men were saying: "We really ought to go over to Tollerdown and see if the others have turned up."

Ross's hair curled like black gorse, Felix's spread like burnt turf. "And not to Starn with me?" she said. A long day off they would have on the turf together; Ross poking about for rare plants, Felix making up a tolerable poem. Ten miles she would walk, also alone in the hills. At the end there would be a point of human life, a station shed a stone's throw from a crazy square, old houses tilted together; the gaping tourists, the market-day beasts; the train poking its head suddenly round an angle in the hills. There she would be eventually accompanied by a stranger, neat, interested, polite.

Then back in a car, flight after the steady walk—which would end where she was now, in a place like a sea-pool, on the lawn grass, in the cool rooms, under the trees, in the wood.

"All right," she said, "I'll go—if you order six lettuces and four lobsters, a basket of currants; and Felix does the flowers." There would be six lobsters and four lettuces. She needed to be alone as much as they.

She took her hat, and ashplant, and left them.

For a while she climbed the green road, worn down in places to its flints, black glass set in white porcelain rings. Below her the field-chequered sea-valley collected a haze. The sea was a hardly visible brilliance. On the top of the down, she looked inland, across another valley to another range, and far inland to Starn on its hill, the hub of the down-wheel, set in its cup of smoke and stone. A very long way over the grass, a very long way down a chalk-road. A longer way through a valley track, called Seven Fields into Starn. Seven Fields, because Felix said there were seven different kinds of enclosures, all unpleasant. A yellow field, a dirty field, a too-wet field, a field where you stubbed your feet. A field with a savage cow, a field with a wicked horse. Always something wrong, whichever way you walked it, except the fourth, which was not a field but an open copse, treed and banked and prettified. 'Midsummer Night's Dream,' true greenwood. And hope, one way, of Starn in a mile and a half. She needed it by the time she reached the copse, in spite of her light stride and airy dress. The boys were off by now, somewhere on Gault cliffs, which was not a nice place, but a wonder and a horror, overhanging a gulf over a wood full of foxes the surf lapped, where even she had never been. The boys would be sitting there, dangling their legs, the gulls fanning them, an unsailable bay under them, transparent, peacock-coloured, where under the water the reefs wound like snakes.

It was all very well. She had told Felix to collect mushrooms and not allow Ross to experiment. He could get them in Ogham meads—What was she worried about? Money, of course, and love affairs; the important, unimportant things. Hitherto God had fed his sparrows, and as good fish had come out of the sea. But everywhere there was a sense of broken continuity, a dis-ease. The end of an age, the beginning of another. Revaluation of values. Phrases that meant something if you could mean them. The meaning of meaning? Discovery of a new value, a different way of apprehending everything. She wished the earth would not suddenly look fragile, as if it was going to start shifting about. Every single piece of appearance. She knew it was only the sun, polishing what it had dried. Including her face, her make-up had made pasty with sweat. There was something wrong with all of them, or with their world. A moment missed, a moment to come. Or not coming. Or either or both. Shove it off on the war; but that did not help.

Only Ross was all right— He never wanted anything that he did not get. Life had given it up and paid over Ross's stakes, because once his strong appetites were satisfied, he did not want anything in human life at all. It was something to eat and drink, to embrace and paint. Apart from that, he knew something that she was only growing conscious of. And wouldn't tell. Not he—laughed at her for not knowing, and for wanting to know.

Felix was quite different. Felix was scared. Fear made him brittle and angry and unjust. Without faith.

Faith was necessary for the knowledge of God. Only, there were fifty good reasons for supporting the non-existence of God. Besides, no one wanted to believe that any more. That was the point. And it was a shame for those two men to make her go all that way through a valley, while they were grubbing about in the wind. The next stile was a beast. She crossed it heavily. A long corner to turn, and there would be Starn to look at. There was that horse again, knotted and stiff and staring at her. It was too far to come. Miles behind her, a white road stood on its head over the hill that led to the green road that led to their house. She had come down that road, a long time ago, turning her back on the sea, to get to Starn, to meet an American, who would like her, not for long, and no one else— Someone had barbed-wired the gap, damn him! She flung herself on her back and wriggled under, jumping up with too great an effort. What was she really doing, out in this burning valley at mid-day? 'They force me with more virtue than is convenient to me. Not innocently— How can we be innocent? I am going to let things go. A witch and a bitch they call me. They shall see.' She flung into the inn at Starn, ashamed of her appearance, red and dusty, and ordered a long drink.

Chapter III

COOL, RESTED, made up, she went to the station. It is always pleasant to collect someone expected out of a train. She wished it had been someone she wanted, someone known or necessary to be known. Michael, who went with the house—Tony, she wished to know better—Vincent, she might get off with—the peacocks of her world. Then she reminded herself of the pleasure it would be to shew a stranger their land, as they knew it, equivocal, exquisite. From what she had observed of Americans, almost certain to be new.

Then she was flying through lanes, an attentive, intelligent old-young man beside her.

"God! What a beautiful place," he said. When 'beautiful' is said, exactly and honestly, there is contact, or there should be. Then, "This is the England we think of. Hardy's country, isn't it?"

"Yes, don't rely too much on the weather and the food."

"Don't worry about me. I've done some camping."

Nice man. But when he stood in the verandah and looked about him, he said: "I couldn't have imagined it."

At tea, he said: "It seems to me that you have everything. No luxury, but all the beauty there is."

Slightly overdoing the beauty business— Beauty is a too concentrated food. And what did he mean about luxury? There was a sort of lean splendour about their things, anyhow. Still, his repose and his careful manners flattered her. She wondered when the men would be back, smelling of turf and thyme, and settle him in. Not a sign of them, and she'd told him they'd gone out to get mushrooms, usually picked at dawn. She took him up to his room and left him. Alone, he sat down on the bed, pensive. "Lord!" he said, "how did I get here?" The properties of the room included a bidet, a chart of the coast, and a still-life of poisonous-looking wood flowers, Felix's work. He thought that the berries were deadly night-shade, which they were. He looked out of the window, the verandah roof sloping beneath him, of slate flags, patched and bound with lichens and ferns, and wondered when and how it had all been put together. His eyes travelled to a yucca, bent like an old man, and opening in a single three-foot spike. Then the wood. He had come out of simple curiosity, and to see something in England off the regulation road. So that was what this Paris bunch did when they got home? What did they do? What was there to do? Where were the men who had asked him? Some kind of trick to leave him alone with the girl?

Getting mushrooms? He decided, for the first time, that mushrooms grew. And that he must carry on, attentively. With immense deliberation the sun was moving west. He stretched his neck out of the window, and saw the crest of the down turn black, and draw up like a tower. He drew in his head. He did not want to see that hill with the stars trembling over it. How did they light the place? *I know moonlight, I know starlight.* Very sensitive to the arts, he admitted that he might soon be justified in singing that. *Lay this body down.* What an idea, but he might soon have to do it. To him, straight from London, Paris, and New York, the silence was intolerable.

The wood sighed at him. Just like that. Two kinds of life he did not want. The ash-fair tree-tall young woman downstairs, and the elaborate piece of leaf and wood, that was one thing and many. The wood and the woman might be interchangeable, and it wasn't the sort of thing you wanted on a visit. He had nerves, too, a great sensibility to take impressions. Always in relation to people. Life to him was an elaborate theatre, without scenery. Here the scenery seemed to be the play.

He got as far as that when he remembered that downstairs there would be certainly something to drink, and began to change, beautifying himself, scrupulously and elaborately as a cat.

He had a cocktail; he had two. A woman came in. Scylla told him she was her old nurse. Was it truth, or a comedy, when she said:

"I found the lobster and the fish Mr. Felix got in the ditch."

And Scylla answered:

"Where are Mr. Felix and Mr. Ross?"

And the nurse had said:

"You never know. I'll bring in dinner."

So they ate together; an eatable meal, fresh-tasting wine, and the inevitable whisky after. A rabbit crossed the lawn. A rat came under the verandah and stole a piece of bread. Two bats flew in. Scylla said:

"They're full of lice, worse luck."

Nothing went on happening: the delicate quiet waited on them.

"I expect," said Scylla, "that they went over to Tollerdown, and found our friends had come to the cottage."

He thought: 'The mushrooms are wearing thin.'
"Where is Tollerdown?"

"One of the hills in this part of the world. You know this country was given its first human character in the late stone age. That's all the earthworks and barrows you see. Two of our friends have a cottage there. They dress up like the Prince of Wales, and quarrel like dogs. It will be fun if they are there."

Well, it might be. Anything which would give Dudley Carston a human scene. And if there was one thing in history one could hope was over, it was the stone age. But the young woman's mind was distracted by the thought of it. She was laughing to herself. Laughing at the stone age. Real, abstract laughter. She had forgotten he was there. That her brother and her friend had disappeared. She might be mad, but she was good-looking. Women lovely and mad, or only lovely and only mad, should not be left alone in woods. Literature did not help him. He could only think of La Belle Dame sans merci, and she wasn't that kind. She should think of him as a real man, not one of her flighty shadows too careless to be there to receive the stranger they had invited to follow them some hundred miles.

"Shall I go and look for them?" he said.

"Where?" she said— That brought it back— "The openness here is deceptive, and they might come a hundred ways. I'm ashamed of their manners."

She was telling herself: 'Something has happened, I think. I told myself this morning I'd watch the scene and not try to make it right. My boy friends can go hang.'

The silence went away, and left nothing.

There was an iron clang. Carston sat tight.

"It's the gate on to the grass," she said, "here they are."

Two heavy men syncopating their walk. Must be a march of trolls in the night through the wood. Nothing natural was coming. Four tall young men crowded into the room.

"So you've collected Carston?"

The men from Tollerdown, of course.

He saw three men about thirty years old. One tall and black, with close-set eyes and a walk affected to hide his strength, called Clarence. One rougher, shorter, fairer, better bred, called Ross. Then a boy, Scylla's brother Felix Taverner, the english peach in flower, lapis-eyes, the gold hair already thinning where the temples should have been thatched. Then, last, the tallest they called Picus, grave as a marsh-bird dancing and as liable to agitation, his colour drawn from the moon's palette, steel gilt and pale, the skin warmed to gold by the weather, cooled to winter in the dark crystal eyes.

Clarence and Picus crowding off to eat in the kitchen. Scylla followed them, but came back.

"Something has happened, I think. If it's what I think it is, it will be a diversion for you."

Not so sure, he waited. They came back. Their fatigue was different from his, an affair of the muscles. They seemed drunk on fresh air. He found himself faced with his usual problem, how to make a fresh event serve his turn, relate it strictly to personalities, especially his own.

That was the situation for him, as he listened, translating, to the story Felix had to tell. Felix said that Ross and he had been to a place called Gault, and he'd sung to it. Presumably a dangerous place. They had then decided to call on distant friends, who might or might not be inhabiting a cottage on a place called Tollerdown. Anyhow, supposing they were not there, a rare species of hawk known as a honey-buzzard might be observed in the vicinity. On arriving they had found their friends (Scylla seemed to be the only woman in the group, a point for reflection) in difficulties owing to their well, shrunk by the drought, yielding nothing but dead hedgehogs. A digression on the use of soda-water to make tea. An excursion down the well to clean out the hedgehogs had led to a discovery. An odd cup of some greenish stone had been found, rather like pea-soup carnelian. The state of the well had necessitated the transfer of Picus and Clarence for an indefinite stay. "You're done in this country if your well gives out. Wait till ours does." Carston was not interested. This might interfere with his making love to Scylla, which he had decided was to be his expression of a successful visit. Unless he found out how to use it.

Then Ross produced the cup suddenly, out of his pocket, and handed it round. Carston said:

"That means nothing to me."

"Been cut by hand," said Felix. "Is there a kind of opaque flint glass? Keltic twiddles, I think, very worn round the rim."

A good deal was told Carston, casually, about Kelts and

Saxons and Romans and early Christianity; things completely over so far as he knew— Not that they talked about what he hadn't heard. Only they talked as if there was no time, no progress, no morality. He knew, of course, that there was no progress, and no morality.

Then Ross said, roughly and softly, as though he was loving something:

"The thing was that we fished it out with a spear."

Scylla said, "Ross, that's odd."

Clarence fidgeted attentively. Felix stared, and Carston saw the boy's tricky brilliant eyes light up. Picus was grave, a man so tall and thin he seemed to go on for ever. Unnaturally supple, he had seen him pick up something behind him as if it had been in front. He tried to think what a spear had to do with it.

Felix said, sharply:

"Good old Freud."

"Idiot!" said Ross, and turned away furious and contemptuous.

"It seems to me," said Scylla, "that people had to start some way of thinking of things. What they saw once they'd learned to think might be quite different from the things they'd learned on."

Then, to Carston, she said that odd things were always happening, and old patterns repeated themselves. That it was sometimes alarming when they did, and Freud very useful in the case of irrational fear. Very true, too, when there had been a row, and no one could feel what was just and what was not. Always look out for the suppressed wish that's taken a wrong turning. But that what had happened to-day was objective and odd.

Carston said:

"I think I'll have to ask you to explain a little more than that."

But Ross had turned round again. "I'm awfully sorry," he said. The insolent insincerity was not meant to be lost on Carston, but it was. "Put it down to the solstice or the heat."

"Tell us the news," said Felix. "We couldn't get back without our tea. Ross believes in perspiration. I don't."

Carston had come with elaborations of the best gossip. They listened to him—rather too attentively, he thought. At the same time there was something that spoiled his effects. It was the place, the faintly lit room mixing with the starlight outside. A shallow little green dish was lying among the glasses. Might have been made out of star-material. The woman had called it a diversion, but they weren't going to let him play. He began suddenly to dislike them, wish to humiliate them. Far too troubled to think how to do it.

Even Ross saw there was something wrong when he left them and went up to bed.

But this Carston had seen. Four ways of saying the woman good-night. Ross nodded to her. Felix embraced her. Clarence kissed her gallantly, with a flourish indicating affectionate indifference to their difference of sex. Picus, busy with a syphon, crooked his fore-finger at her across the room.

Chapter IV

T HE MORNING RESTORED Carston to kinder thoughts.
Last night might have been spent under the sea. If
they had drawn him down, it was possible that they had
not done it intentionally. His room was comfortable, if
mad, full of little bits out of the sea. A ship in a bottle
pleased him. On a hook was an old cap with an anchor. A
ship was painted inside his morning cup of tea.

After breakfast he had the sea full; bathing with Felix
who treated the sea like a living animal. Carston was content to show how well he swam. Very content, that he swam
so well, better than the boy. Looking from the rocks inland, he thought it might really be quite all right if there
was not too much scenery that called for a too high quality
of attention. At least he could not go back next day. Pride
forbade it. He must stay until he had some power over
them. That would be his compensation for a week's bore-
dom and acquit him.

Scylla he was reconsidering. To make love to her
would be too hard work, too easy. The sort of woman who
forgot all about you next day.

To have power at a moment's notice, it is as well to
begin by knowing a secret. He remembered the cup still
on the table at breakfast, and used by Ross as an ash-tray.
Then, that Felix had not used it.

"You know," he said to the boy, "that I was very interested in what you were saying last night. But I didn't quite
catch on."

Felix was thinking that here was something nice and
new, who did the things they did, a little differently. With
the fundamental error that being an American, simplicity

and kindness would be his chief characteristic. He surprised Carston with his quickness to explain.—"We got over there, and found Picus saying he was ill and Clarence doing all the work. As usual. So, after tea with soda water, I went down in the bucket. The others hung on to the windlass and Picus strolled out. Got a fishing spear with him, because he said high hedgehogs aren't things to handle (they smell water and fall in, poor brutes). I raised that cup along with the corpses. We were looking at it, and Picus began to whistle. You must hear him whistle; it's like Mozart. Said he was perfectly well again. He and Ross are mighty queer birds."

"Tell me more about your friends."

"Picus is Clarence's 'old man of the sea' only he's young. Clarence doesn't know it. Scylla says I'm hers. He only does one or two small things like whistling, but he does them perfectly. Riding and blowing birds' eggs. You saw how powerful his body is, but he's like a bird. Off in a flash. Hence the name. Picus was the Woodpecker.

"Clarence fights for him and with him. What he fights for, I don't know. Clarence is quite all right. A bit insincere, because he's afraid. And what he's afraid of, I don't know."

Carston could only say: "Tell me more."

"Scylla's a different egg. If there is anything wrong about my sister, it's everything. I've said the word 'fear' at least ten times lately. This time it's my own." He horrified Carston—he was like a desperate butterfly, angry, petulant and white.—"It's she at one end, and Picus at the other, who get me going. It's because she wants everything to happen to its last possibility. That's how she gets kick out of life. Once a thing's got going, she'll understand it and manage it. And enjoy it. She'll never tone it down. Sort of woman who'd have mothered the house of Atreus, and though I owe her everything, it's wasted on me. She'll enjoy—"

"What will she enjoy?"

"What will happen out of what happened yesterday. Don't you see. That infernal Picus is a psychic if there ever was one. Or if there is such a thing."

"Does she believe in that?"

"Believing doesn't trouble her. Only what is going to happen. She doesn't create situations. She broods them and they hatch. And the birds come home to roost. Some mighty queer birds. Truth isn't everyone's breakfast egg. She isn't happy till it's hatched. Calls it knowing where you are. I wish I knew where I was—"

Carston revised his ideas again about Scylla as a lover. He could only say: "But what can she and your friend Picus make out of what happened yesterday, anyhow?"

"Don't you see? It was fishing it out of the well with that old spear—they always went together."

"What went with what?"

"The cup of the Sanc-Grail, of course. It and the spear, they always hunted in couples. You've heard of it. All sexual symbolism. I wish I hadn't."

"Does sexual symbolism get you?" It would be news if it did.

"I should worry. But the Sanc-Grail was a very funny thing. People used to think it was a shallow greenish dish. And the cup's a shallow, greenish dish. Those well-shafts on the downs might be any age. So might it. Tollerdown had a bad reputation, and I never heard of the Sanc-Grail doing anyone any good. With that moron Picus behind it, and that demon, my sister, in front of it."

Carston took stock of several things: what he remembered of the Grail story, the possibility of anyone behaving as if it had happened, and what that implied in human character. Felix's youth.

He said at last:

"Don't tell me your sister is superstitious."

"Not she. Better if she was. She'd read it up and do processions and things. It might be like that. But with her it won't get its home comforts. It will get vision."

On the last four words he changed, and Carston saw the sister in the brother, in the elegant, frightened boy now explaining that what he wanted was not vision, but fashionable routine.

"Of course, there is nothing in it. I only meant that the find's a reminder."

"Reminder of what?"

"Of what it would remind you, of course. Oh! I see you don't know. Never mind, it's a long story."

Carston gave out. He was not pleased. He had been atrociously taken into confidence, and he had not understood. His earlier dislike of them returned, with an uncomfortable respect. The Sanc-Grail did not call on everybody. The boy was a young thing, telling him how much he hated poverty and dreams. What a snob he was. All about the things you could not do. Felix remembered that Ross had prepared them to be misunderstood. It did not occur to him that he had no right to expect that Carston should understand.

Chapter V

PICUS WAS ALONE in his room, modelling the body of
Scylla in wax. One of the little things he did. Clarence
was a serious and accomplished painter, discovered and
produced by Ross. Picus played about with wax, which
grew more transparent as he touched it. Exceedingly powerful in body, he looked like wax, in a gauze-thin blue
sweater rolled up his neck. He looked out of the window
at the wood swimming in the mid-day heat, let out a little
breath and waited an answer from the wood. He smiled
and began to dance, like a marsh-bird, swinging up a leg,
effortlessly, in any direction.

Then his face expressed pain. He put up his hands to
his head and pressed them in. In a kind of despair, he
turned and dug his nails in the wax of Scylla's flesh.

Carston came upstairs to wash, bewildered by the dark
stair, the corridor crossed with sun motes. He walked into
Picus's room by mistake. There he saw him, very gracious,
in a room shabbier than his own, making the portrait of
Scylla in wax. He saw brightness, nakedness, a toy. A liveli-
ness of colour to remind him that she was a young woman
alone among young men.

"I don't like it," said Picus, and broke it.—"I'll make
another after tea." Carston could have cried. The waste
of richness, the shocking petulance, a toy that excited him
shewn and taken away. For a moment he had embraced
Scylla. Another of the little things they did in their spare
time.

Pushed out of his politeness, he said:

"You're the one who discovered the cup, aren't you?"

"No," said Picus, "I only thought of the spear to poke
about with. It was Felix's find."

"Miss Taverner's brother seems a bit upset about it."

"Does he?"

"You shouldn't have broken that statue."

Picus covered up both statements like a perfect young gentleman, rather a stupid one. It occurred to Carston that he was stupid; also that perhaps it had scandalised him to have shewn Scylla naked to a stranger, and hoped it was that.

They went down to lunch. It was his first lunch, but he felt as though never in his life had he done anything but eat there. Once he had lived in America, once he had come to Europe, but that did not count any more. That theatre was as another earth, and the plays were not the prologue to his play. For this play there had been no re-hearsal and he did not know his part. Or, if he had a part, he had to improvise it, and it must be a good part. Lost in a green transparent world, he was blind. Beginning to see in a new way he disliked, a seeing like jealousy, without arrangement; principally a sensibility about Scylla, likely to become a fury of desire. He remembered its modest beginnings the night before, his rejection of it on further acquaintance with her brother. That it had started again in Picus. Somebody said: "What do we do this afternoon?" The heat answered that. Laid down on the verandah in a wicker chair like a shell, he lay still, face to face with the wood. One by one the others disappeared.

* * * * *

Ross went up the hill, carrying his painting things. The place he wanted could not be seen from any shade there was on the down-top. He planted his easel in the full light.

The cliffs down the coast were too good-looking. He chose the somberest patch of barn and field in the next valley and drew it hard, his shirt-sleeves rolled up his am-ber arms, his back square to the house in the wood, several hundred feet together.

Presently he noticed that it was becoming difficult always to distinguish between a sheep and a shrub, and that that meant thunder. With his back to the house and the wood he was being stopped working from the other side. He drew in a tree-shape rather hard. The white haze gathered. The more he looked, the less he saw. Instead, he began to see shapes in his head, not outside it, an exercise he avoided, because it interfered with precision of hand. Unwillingly he felt that he would have to return before he meant to, to a place where there was a martyred ass called Clarence, lying alone for a moment in a verandah, a little distance from a young American, who was keeping remarkably silent. Whom his instincts were against. Not because he disliked him, but because the town-bred contact between them had died. They were all stuck down there in a bewilderment, which had happened because they had forgotten the duties of hospitality and had left it to Scylla to fetch the stranger from Starn. If they had not done that, two of the party would have died of the hedgehogs, or else come straight over to them without raking up a well. Not that he was sorry that it had happened. Then he whistled as he drew, out of tune, but as though he was loving something. No nonsense about being the thing he loved, but like a lover, aware of the presence of what he loved everywhere.

There was a hard, explosive sound. Several mixed noises. A bird tore out of a thicket and crossed an open space, indirectly, frantically, and disappeared. He imitated its call and burst out laughing. "Woodpecker up to his tricks again." Then he went back to his work, straining his eyes.

* * * * *

In the verandah, Clarence slept. He dreamed that he was walking, at night, on a thin spit of rock across the sea, Picus's slender height and great weight against his shoulders, in his arms. Picus was dead, and he was glad he was dead and it was over. The difficulty was to get rid of the body, which was coming alive somewhere else and following him. It could only be got rid of at the end of the rock, and he could not go on much longer like that. There were dark hills round the sea, and in them was the living Picus, not his at all, but another, the real one. It was such a bother, his feet were covered with blood. It wasn't till the dead Picus was in the sea, that the real one would come out of the hills and play with him. No use waiting for day, because it was always dark in that country.

He often went there when he was asleep, often with a dead bird, Picus the Woodpecker, in his hand and in his arms. Sometimes it was an image for Picus. Sometimes him. There came a point when he would say: "This is a play, made out of my wishes and my disappointment. Truth is quite different. I am unhappy because the boy has things wrong with his character, because he has things wrong with his inside. Or, because we all think, somehow, that Picus is a bad lot." After this correction there would come the final idea that saw behind these images and their rationalisation another truth. He stirred, shifted and fell asleep again, not knowing at all that Carston, awake, was wondering why he seemed so wretched, and why he had dictated them and taken offence at lunch. That Carston liked him, and admired his good looks, who could only see how worn they were beside the American's ageless set trimness.

He dreamt again: another Picus came walking up the rock-spit, carrying a glass dish which was the cup of the Sanc-Grail, saying: "It's the *lapis exilii,* the stone of exile. What I'm walking on is the *lapis exilis,* the slender stone. All the same, my dear." Then the neat reminder that no grail texts were clear what the thing was really called. Then his private fancy to call it the *lapis exultationis,* the stone of joy. That the thing had never existed. The joy-stone. Freud again. Had he ordered more wax for Picus to play with? A letter with a stamp like a black star, shifting along a river which carried the London post. Too slowly. It must get there quick, or Picus would be angry and say he hadn't sent it. He woke to remember that that had been an old quarrel, and the stuff had come. Also that he ought to talk to Carston, wide awake in a basket chair, five stone pillars away. That he was feeling horribly shy, raw, ill-adjusted, sick to assure himself that the others thought he was good for something. Had the American seen through him? After all, he'd seen war. Half an hour's more sleep. Perhaps the dreams would be more comfortable, or wouldn't come.

Carston was wondering if he was expected to come over and talk. He liked to hear Clarence talk about war. He had seen some rough stuff himself in Russia. A good soldier the man must have been. Wondered why he hadn't stuck to it, and was now rather overdoing the art business. The others did not overdo it. Quite a good painter, too. Then he saw Scylla in the tree-tops. A limb of ilex, detached from the main height and formed perfectly. Lifted up, glittering in the insolent sky. She was upstairs, broken in pieces, in preposterously pretty, sexual wax. Picus might be there, making another. He'd go up and see. Creep in, if he wasn't allowed to enjoy it.

Almost as good as having the girl, to have that thing of her in wax. This was as far as he got. It was quite true that the statue would have done as well. Desire in Carston was almost mental, a redecoration of his memories. Only at the moment he was between the two, the statuette and the girl, the shoulders he saw in leaf and wax and flesh, and was troubled by the repeats.

While Clarence, asleep again, dreamed he was meeting Picus as he had met him in the war, wearing his shrapnel helmet, a queer glass dish someone had found in a well. Rather a worry.

"Big magic," said Picus. He was a boy then, his smile already gracious and timid, contrasting with a loose, haughty walk. He had said, laughing: "If you take it off,

off comes my hair." That was important. The queer fairy
cup his bird wore. Some day Picus would take off his cap
to him. He woke up. Something had broken in him, the
sense of wrong adjustment was easier. It would come back,
but now it was perfectly easy to talk to Carston, by this
time also anxious to bridge the gulf between lunch and tea.

Chapter VI

TEA WAS a reasonable meal, with a real human being at it, the doctor having come over from Starn to attend to Picus's health. Carston held his attention, improvising brilliantly on aspects of his native land, wondering if he could interpret Scylla's cordiality into the beginnings of desire. Quick work, he knew, but life in the infernal stillness was going at a pace that had New York beat. It became the doctor's turn to talk. Carston noticed how they played in turns, the second guest after the first. "Pass the buns," said Felix. That was the cue. Carston listened to stories of medical practice in a remote district; after a time to an accompaniment he did not at first locate. Later that it was Picus ringing with a spoon on his medicine glass.

The doctor said:

"I don't wonder you two left Tollerdown. It's a cheerless place at best. I only knew it in winter, going out there to deliver the shepherd's wife. So I think of it as the darkest place that exists."

Scylla answered: "I know. Even now when it is burnt white. I think of it the only time I was there in winter, in a storm. Wind roaring over the flint-crop and snow whirling. Lying an instant and vanishing."

Ross said: "BE PREPARED FOR LAMBING—You hear them mewing in the dark, and see a light in a wooden box on wheels, and out comes a shepherd, with his hands covered with blood."

The doctor said:

"Shew me the cup you got out of the well." And when he had looked at it: "The luck of the country's with you. I'm glad to find a few roman pots. It isn't glass at all, too heavy. I think it's jade. It may have been set once. I tell

•28•

you, it might have been the cup of a chalice." Intelligent interest. Carston felt quite friendly now towards the thing. The others were giving polite attention. Five people at once thinking about a spear. No, six. He was.

"One has time to remember things, shooting about this country in a Ford. Do you know it makes me think of what I remember of the cup of the Sanc-Grail?"

Picus said, meekly: "What was that?"

Carston thought: 'How was that camp, or wasn't it? Would one of them pick up the challenge? Of course, it was a challenge.' Ross said: "That's a long story," but Scylla leaned forward, excited, and said: "The best way to get that story out is for everyone to say what he thinks or feels or remembers. The Freud game really. Start, Felix!"

"Tennyson," said Felix.

"Oh, my dear," said Clarence, "those awful pre-Raphaelite pictures put me off it long ago."

Ross said: "A mass said at Corbenic."

"Wagner," said the doctor.

"A girl carrying it," said Carston, staring at Scylla and trying to play.

Scylla said: "*Quod inferius, sicut superius est.*"

Picus said: "You haven't told me much."

"Second round," said Scylla,—"people enlarge on what they said before."

"I said Tennyson," said Felix, "because I hate the Keltic Twilight. And nearly all its works. I hate it because it's a false way of telling about something that exists. No, a messy way. Responsible for the world's worst art. Now and then it nearly comes off. Milton left it alone, and I don't blame him. Tennyson made it idiotic with his temperance knights. Fixed it, too, enough for parody. Killed the unstated thing which I don't mind telling you scares me."

Clarence said: "I agree with Felix. I can't stand bad drawing."

Ross said: "At Corbenic, wherever that was, there was a different mass. It may have been the real thing."

The doctor said: "Parsival is like a great religious service to me."

Carston, embarrassed at his turn coming, saw their pained faces. He said: "I supposed the girl who carried it was the female spirit of life."

Scylla said: "I quote again: *'Here lies the Woodpecker who was Zeus.'*"

"Thank you," said Picus.

Later, Carston asked her to take him for a walk. The doctor went with them to the gate, and she asked him what he thought about Picus's health.

"Everything is wrong, and nothing," he said. —"I don't mean by that that he invents it. His aches and pains are a mask that conceals something. What that is, I've never been able to find out—"

"Does Clarence know?"

"I shouldn't care myself to know too much about Picus. Despair's a bad bedfellow."

Scylla said: "We know what despair is." As if she were saying that she knew how to take a temperature. Carston went with her down the wood to the sea. Twenty-four hours before he had been alone with her for the first time. Alone with her the second time, he was almost in pain because he wished to use the moment, and did not know how. The more he planned the less he'd be able to do, who had rarely failed with women. Now the sun struck aslant, the light-chequers broadened into patches. It was damp and delicious. The evening birds were tuning up. A little sympathy is generally judicious.

"I took a walk this morning with your brother. He seemed troubled by what you found yesterday. Even now, after the talk at tea, I'm not clear what it is all about."

Not a hint of his sex had crossed her mind. An american boy, very polished and friendly. No reason not to tell him anything there was to tell.

For the third time Carston heard the sentence: "That's a long story. You must help me to explain."

He answered: "You said two things at tea. The Latin bit, which means, I think, that the things underneath are the same as the things on top. And something I don't get at all: '*Here lies the Woodpecker who was Zeus.*'"

"Yes."

"Then you said another thing—you said that you all knew what despair is. How can that be true?"

Scylla said: "Well, I take it that we have to know everything about being lost."

Lost. He did not get that. If ever there existed a group sure of themselves. He mentioned it.

"Swank," she said, "and instinct. To cover quite intolerable pain. You see we know between us pretty well all there is to know. That's why we rag all the time. To keep things clean, and because it's the only gentlemanly thing to do. We have our jokes, our senses, and our moments of illumination which always take a turn for the worse. See? We live fast and are always having adventures, adventures which are like patterns of another adventure going on somewhere else all the time. A very different sort of affair, a state suggested if you like in a good work of art. The things down here seem hints of it, but there is nothing to make us sure that it is a reality. Let alone that it is worth what it costs us. Quite the contrary. We get into trouble over it, it runs after us, runs away from us, runs away with us, makes fun of us and fools of us. Because of it we have no money, and the wrong lovers, and our instinct for power is starved. For we come of families which have never been without power before. And the name for all this is our subconscious minds. And between Freud and Aquinas, I've managed to tell you about it completely wrong. For another of its names is intellectual beauty, and another, the peace of God."

"D'you believe in God?"

"I don't know. All we do know is what happens to faith based on catch-as-catch-can visions."

"Weren't all religions based on that?"

"They were, and look at them! But now you see why
we felt we were being laughed at, dangerously, when we
lifted that cup out of a well on the point of a spear?"

Carston pulled himself together. "What did you mean
by the other thing: *'Here lies the Woodpecker who was Zeus'*?"

"A little poetry, a little witchery, a little joke. It's the
same thing as I said before. Now I'll tell you something
worse than what I said before.

"Along with faith fit for people like us, and good taste
which are where morals end, there is no goodwill left anywhere in the world. Which started to go first, or if they all
went together, or which pushed the other out, I don't
know. I've an idea that something else, a principal we
haven't named yet, got rid of the lot."

Beginnings for an erotic conversation.

A turn of exasperation seized him. She was leaning on
the red arm of a pine tree which stood by itself outside the
wood, a crooked blue mushroom moulded by the wind.
The scent from its cap mixed with the smell of wind off
the tide-stripped rocks.

"Now you see why that cup upset Felix? If it is anything, it is only a Keltic mass-cup. And that, perhaps, is
not certain. I don't think you do see. As Felix would say:
'I don't blame you.' But an american poet said: *'Memory,
you have the key.'*"

"I have no memories," said Carston.

"We are all wishing we hadn't; because memory produces imagination, and imagination is a state by itself.
Memory was the Muses' mother, and the muses are nine
names of the imagination. I told you you'd see some fun.
Now I must go over to the coast-guards and order a car.
We want to take you somewhere to-morrow. See the thunder clouds banking up? I must get back before the rain."

Carston thought: 'Getting rid of me. In an instant she
would be off like a hare.' He said:

"Stay a minute. Maybe it's because I have no memories,
but I don't see where the fun comes in."

"Don't you call it fun to watch how violently, strangely and in character people will behave? Watch Ross, watch Clarence. Watch me." He was watching her. Green, pointed feet in plaited shoes, bare arms, pointed breasts under a dress full of air. *Blow away the morning dew.* That was remembering something. Like open fir-cones dipped in fire and cream, the thunder-clouds were piling up the sky. Mounting the hills, a wing of them rising out of the sea. Inshore, a breath of wind clashed the pine needles.

Another memory.

Love only me.

Donna Lombarda.

Love only me.

Love only me. Because the tune was what the needles brushed out, and the words the wish that made his body ache.

"Can I come with you?"

She looked at him candidly. She wanted to be alone. "I must go to the farm as well; I do the housekeeping at this time. It's a hot flat walk. The others have gone down to the rocks to fetch a drift-wood log. If you liked to help them to get it up. It's bleached white, and when it burns it will go up in blue and green sparks." He saw that there was something pathetic in the way they made a game of their poverty.

"I'll go to them," he said, "but you haven't explained what the american poet meant when he said that memory had the key?" She had moved away from him.

"He said:

> *Mount.....*
> *Put your shoes at the door,*
> *Sleep, prepare for life.*

And called it: *The last twist of the knife.* Adieu."

The log, as he expected, was large and most unwilling to be moved; the cliff-path more a gesture in broken clay than an ascent.

He saw her in his mind, dew blowing away over burnt, empty grass towards a formidable other world, its edges drawn in fire, the thunder-clouds now half-way across the sky.

Before dinner, he remembered the library, the middle room of the house. Alone there, he looked for something, not Tennyson, to enlighten him. He found a book, and sat in a window with it. Presently he noticed the entrance, one after the other, of Clarence, Felix, and Ross, and that they all went, reticently but eventually, to the same gap in the shelves.

Chapter VII

THEY DINED WITHOUT Picus or Scylla. He saw Clarence, uneasy, and heard that Picus had gone out alone because the doctor had told him to take walks. The earth was now closed in a hot, purple air-ball, the lightning flicking on and off. Without any regard for the weather, Ross arranged their chairs in the verandah while the storm banged about. Carston was silent. He was not accustomed to invite the lightning to visit him under trees. And Clarence seemed fatuous to him when he turned on the gramophone to play against the sky. They were not disturbed about Scylla, who might be out walking alone in the livid night. Apparently the farmer had an old father who gave her beer and told her ghost stories. It was Clarence who swung up and down, turning disks, and saying teasings that were brittle and raw, in his rich, sad voice, tortured and made petulant by the uproar through which his friend's feet could not be heard coming through the wood.

Carston thought that it was like the place to leap up from its equivocal quiet into an orgy of cracking and banging. He wanted to go and meet Scylla. To see her safely home. Why were they so careless of their women? She had told him that love had left them. Had courtesy? She might come a hundred ways. It was the same as on the night when the men had been lost. They had come back safe from adventure. He wanted her to enter with him. He was an american gentleman in an uneasy place. Yes, he would go at once and fetch his young hostess. A proper thing to do. He felt at ease for the first time.

Ross advised not: "She knows her way. You'd never find it. It will rain in a minute. You'll see to-morrow morning the freshest earth there is."

*"Prepare for life,
The last twist of the knife."*

For the freshest earth there is. 'Phat' went a raindrop on a flag, and a double uproar began. For an hour it rained, through sheet lightning, and thunder like a departing train, the hills calling to one another. The gutters of the roof rushed and sang and leaked, single notes from which the ear eventually picked out a tune. Syncopation, magic, nature imitating Mozart? Carston came to hear it as an overture, for some private earth-life, mercifully and tiresomely apart from his.

Things going on singing, not to him. Escaping also, not finishing, or finishing somewhere else. Beginning again, to enchant him with fragments. He admitted that he was enchanted— When would Scylla wind up the charm by coming through the wood?

The storm tuned up again, the rain striking in rods, filling the air with fine spray. The others were enjoying it, the first row of the stalls for a nature-play. Discussing other spectacles. Then he saw Scylla and Picus run out of the wood and across the lawn, laughing, wet as dogs. He heard Clarence order Picus upstairs to change, to be ignored, while Scylla squeezed out her hair.

"We ran back together. It was too good to miss. Tell me, Carston, does the lightning get you when you're under a tree, or when you're not? We tried both."

That was all there was to it. But how had they met? All prearranged he supposed. No, Picus had done it. Loped off another way to meet her at the farm. She was saying: "You're lucky that you didn't come with me. Admit you'd have hated it?" Was that flirting with him? He asked her what she meant. "Storms aren't in your schedule." So wet they both seemed naked. They all went in. He made hot grog for her over the wood fire, the acid smoke bringing water to his eyes. They looked like real tears to Ross, who wondered. Scylla came down in blue, her hair tied up in a gold cloth, unable to stop laughing. Clarence followed her. Ross said: "Got Picus to bed?"

"No: insists on shaving, and to spite me stands about in his skin." There was more behind what he said than self-pity, yet Carston felt that Clarence had better have hit them in his exasperation than have pitied himself. Why, he wondered? Scylla had said that goodwill had left the earth, but he had noticed that they were compassionate. Perhaps it was that they knew pity's value and feared a sudden demand. At the same time he had no sympathy for Clarence, and they had, who were looking askance at him as though he had said a tactless obscenity. Scylla was saying:

"Warm inside and out. Carston, you're sound on grog."

Picus came down, flushed and transparent, and asked him for some. He found that he could not say 'Help yourself,' forced to wait on him.

"Let's dance," said Scylla; and they danced together, the six of them, but Picus infinitely the best. One of the little things he could do, but not one with Scylla, who moved about with her brother, limbs of the same tree.

There were only five glasses when they all wanted drinks—Picus came over with the cup for Clarence to fill with whiskey and soda. "I don't mind using the ash-tray," he said; and Carston heard through the jazz and the slackening rain a voice which might have been a woman's or a man's: "He doesn't mind using the cup of the Sanc-Grail for whiskey and soda," and another voice, which might have been a man's or a woman's: "He doesn't mind using for a whisky and soda, the cup we use for an ash-tray, the cup of the Sanc-Grail."

The last of the lightning winked at them, the rain turned to a sweet shower, an after-thought.

What'll I do? the gramophone was saying: *What'll I do, what'll I do?* Make love to Scylla, thought Carston. Hadn't they ever thought of that? Shew then that they had among

them a living cup. He remembered the new records he had
brought them from London, and went upstairs to fetch
them. Outside Picus's door he remembered. They were
making a noise downstairs. He could look in. More Scylla.
A whip-up for senses which were, perhaps, older than
theirs. Not refreshed—he thought of it with a sneer—by
memories and the past. They should create his memories
for him.

He fetched the records, and, a little elated by drink,
opened the door of Picus's room. The draught from the
window made his candle stream. He saved it and looked.
There was no statuette. Even the broken pieces had been
cleared away. His light under control, he looked round.
Clothes in exquisite order, chaste, ivory dressing things in
rows. Scent bottles with a silver strainer, a hollowed bunch
of grapes. Nothing to read. Like Ross there. The other
went about weighted with books. Something to read.
Somebody's book on early church vessels. So Picus had a
rationalist mind? Not much read. Time to go.

Below, he was greeted with cheers.

Airs went to his head.

> *Waiting for the moon to rise and shew me the way*
> *To get you to say*
> *I love you.*

"Will there be a moon, soon?" he asked Ross—"after
the storm, I mean?"

"Sorry; she's over. To do her tricks, I mean. Aldebaran's very bright just now."

Damn the stars. *I know starlight.* And the penalty. Leave
the stars to them. Carston turned a disk: "I think you'll
like this. Not come to London yet."

They did. Incarnated him responsible for *O Lady be
good*, as for everything else in America. Scylla, dancing
with him, smiled as he sang *I've been so awfully misunderstood*, with candour, with friendship, with something spilt
over from a reserve of joy. He derided the men because
not one of them knew what she was, because an American

would discover a treasure worth a hundred Sanc-Grails.
There was Picus dancing about like a marsh-bird courting,
with an old cup on his head. Up and down and sideways,
and never a drop spilt. Tilted his head sideways and
caught it as it fell, and it was empty all the time. "Now I
call that cheating." In a moment it was back again and full,
and never a drop was spilt.

Then Carston showed them the Charleston, and tumbled with them up to bed, shaking hands at doors, easy at
last, and full of goodwill.

The air that filled his room was moist and strong,
preparation for the freshest earth there is. The elation
went out of him and left content. The visit had given him
wonder. That was good, because one got brittle and lonely
travelling round, and quick to mistrust. How simple it had
been to win on these lordly young men. Love their women.
Their place was his now. And the wood. It stood like something punished under the rain. He blew out his candle,
and lay down in bed.

A minute later the tail of the lightning winked. The
rain quickened. The door next his opened. The gutter
outside began to run fast again. Through the finale of the
storm, he heard a gull crying. Then, outside his door he
heard a whistle like a glass flute. How loud, how long he
could not judge, startled by it, teased by it. It was outside
the door where Scylla slept. All he could do was repeat the
words of the call, as it poured out, with grace notes and
repeats:

> *Oh, sweet and lovely lady be good,*
> *Oh, lady, be good to me.*
> *I've been so awfully misunderstood,*
> *So, lady, be good to me.*
> *Oh, lady, please have pity,*
> *I'm all alone in this great city,*
> *I'm just a lonely babe in the wood,*
> *So, lady, be good to me.*

Scylla's door opened, neither noisily nor stealthily. Carston was out of bed, his ear to a split panel. He heard her laugh, her stage notion of an american accent. "I should worry." Her door shut. He felt like a weight on his body, the three feet of stone between them. On the other side of that they were lying together, in the quiet of the wood. After a time, he went to the window to listen. But only the casement farthest from him was open, and there was no light. Shocked, almost whimpering, he went back to bed, falling, thanks to the strong air, very quickly asleep. Outside, the night cleared. Over the wood Orion hung up his belt and sword. In the pommel, Aldebaran shook; the star some time before Ross had offered to his attention.

Chapter VIII

THE MORNING was a merciful bustle, with Ross's promise come true of the freshest earth there is. The car arrived, and there seemed to be a controversy where they were to go. To pay a call or see some antiquity. Felix put his foot down on the antiquities.

Carston saw Scylla, preoccupied, perfectly and hideously gay.

They took him to Starn and shewed it him: as if it was a live thing; and did not notice that he resented its life, and was making attempts to kill it. Principally he remembered it because it was half full of people from the world outside. Not peasants, people in vulgar clothes, on motorcycles, in Ford cars, come to stare because it was summer, whom his party treated as if they were a disease.

After lunch the object of the expedition leaked out. He was told that there was a farm, some way off, where mead was made and could be bought. The price of whisky and drinkable wine had turned their thoughts to it. There was no road to the farm. About the distance they were delicately indefinite. They spoke about a track across a place they called the Heath.

Carston had seen the Heath, had crawled along it for miles in the train. It had seemed purple and endless, and he suspected full of traps. The other side of these people's world of hills and the sea. Their idea was that it was time for Carston to visit it, covered with a gauze of every variety of heather, the sweet blood-bright burning crop out of which the honey wine was made.

They rested a little and set out.

Ross caught up Scylla, walking ahead, picking out the track. "A word with you," he said, "don't let anyone know."

"Why not?"

"Because of the American, because of Felix, because of Clarence."

"Why shouldn't they know that Picus and I have an amourette and have magic between us?"

"There's something wrong to-day with Carston."

"At worst he'll leave and blast my reputation for a bit. What of that? And, anyhow, how did you find out, a floor up with Felix and Clarence?"

"Felix and Clarence snoring. Carston quiet, Picus whistling."

"Ross, why have that tall bird and I become lovers? I want to know that. I think it is the kind of thing we shall find out about when it's over, and wonder at." Ross said:

"There is trouble about. The kind that comes with brightness. Can you see that?"

"I can," she said. "Do you mean that Picus is up to no good? I rather agree."

"The first rule," said Ross, "is that Picus is never up to any good."

"Allow me a little fantasy about him."

"Remember that I told you."

"You are being one of the enemies of the rose. Why should you? You always do what you like. Leave that to Clarence."

"I'm telling you to be careful."

"Are we never to have any peace, only adventure and pain? And you, Ross, have a sacred peace."

"So have you. It's the others. That's why they had better not know."

"Perhaps not Felix. Brothers will be brothers."

"Carston's bored. To-day he's upset. Satan's looking for a job for him. I think you were to have been the job."

"First I've heard of it."

"We didn't tell him how long he was to stay."

"You mean that our 'come down and see us' is going to add an episode to what Felix calls the family horror?"

"I mean that anything that's going to happen that shouldn't will find him useful to happen through. Also, a thing you will be too vain to see. This is a move against Clarence by your fancy-boy."

She looked across the purple land to where it ended in the waters of an estuary, more transparent than the sky. "Remember what has to be remembered, too—that Picus and I are young and handsome, rather in love. That he is full of fun and dancing, and bird-calls. Like I am. These things count as well."

"You'll see."

"You are not counting on me?"

"If you can keep things steady, you'd better."

"Perhaps I'm tired of keeping things steady for you. This is my pleasure and my game. And Clarence is unreasonable. Think of it another way, Ross: that Picus is giving us an excuse for the sacred game."

He answered sullenly: "Americans are bad players. At bridge or gardening, or life; especially when it is life as the sacred game. And it isn't his game here, anyhow."

Scylla said: "I'll tell you something. Picus doesn't want Clarence to know. He's afraid of that."

"So he should be. Where would he be without him?"

"Dead, perhaps. That's why I'll do my best to be decent. And now, I want you to tell me what you think about the cup?" He turned away and beat the heather with his stick.

"It's too late, Ross, to be petulant, because you know too much or too little. When you said there was trouble about like brightness, you spoke of things which are nefast, and you've got to go on. Remember Freud."

"We aren't worthy," he cried.

"Worthy? What's worthy? Was anyone? And you've forgotten Gawaine, the knight of the world and of courtesy."

"I didn't know he came into it."

"That comes of never opening a book."

"I detest women."

"Never mind detesting me, which is what you mean. If that cup is anything at all, if it was once an old cup of the sacrament people called 'big magic,' if it's anything or nothing, we can't hurt it, and it can't hurt us. We have our courage and our imagination. We have to be as subtle as our memories. That's all. And but one thing: Picus has given the cup to me."

"Considering your relations, I suppose he had to."

"Then forward, damsel of the Sanc-Grail."

"How dare you!" said Ross, "how dare you!"

She looked at him stoically, "I thought better of you, Ross. Thought there was something hard and great in you. I'm tired of being disappointed. Hear the words of the lover of a bird. He is light and winged and holy. And I mean by holy all there can be in the word; I mean, tabu. You are heavy, wingless, and sacred. And you are a very sensual man. You should understand."

"I understand that you're up in risky air, because you've got off with the worst of the lot of us."

"I can fly." She waited a moment and then spoke cheerfully: "The first thing I understand is that you and I are being unpleasant to each other. The difficulty in this business will be to see the obvious. If Picus is up to his tricks, he's won the first round. And I've tried to pretend that Picus means less than he does to me. To please you, and because it sounds chic. I take that back. And we shall all see."

Ross stood still, his face wrinkled like a pony, sniffing.

"Where are they?" he said. They looked back over magenta risings, yellow sand-holes, black bunches of trees. Quite different from the ravishing gauze seen from Starn on its hill. They waited, but neither one body nor four could be seen moving out of a pocket or over a ridge of the huge, broken honeycomb. Scylla said:

"Has Carston got lost?"

Ross did not suppress a laugh. "He's got three of us with him."

"We're not heath-people."

"Picus knows it. Spends days prowling about here." That subject, delicately picked up, was dropped. "Let's get on."

"No, let's wait."

"Why should we?"

"Because of the mead. Think of us, sweating back with a dozen between us."

Bing. A large black bee slapped Ross's cheek and swung out along the ribbon of sand-path across which the heather stalks whipped their ankles.

"Follow the bee," he said, "it won't be the last walk we shall take together."

"Good!" she said—"at worst they will only be lost. Who minds being lost when there is so much to see? They can steer by Starn. We'll collect what we can, and get home with some martyrdom in hand."

For the last time she looked back over the blazing plain from which an army might pop out. Ross did not look back. He stood with his head flung up, his mouth stretching into its wild-animal smile. With violent, silent amusement, he said:

"It's beginning."

Chapter IX

A T A CHOICE of tracks apparently parallel and similar, Picus had led them to the left. He had trooped them through a wood and sweated them over a crest, to drop them again in a sunk road, made for running contraband a century before. He was asking: "Where are the others?"

"I want my mead," said Felix. "The farm's ahead on the water's edge, where the heath runs out in a point."

Sunk roads are filled with loose sand. They go from nowhere to nowhere now. They trap the sun and keep out air. Their banks curl over in a fringe of heather wire. Adders bask on their striped sides. From this one Starn was invisible, and the eventual blue water bright as dew.

Carston plodded beside Clarence, his feet chafing with sand. They left the wood and crossed another ridge, and saw on their right a creek of yellow grass running inland behind them. They walked another mile till they came to the base of the point, and saw cottages under a crest of dark land. Felix cried out: "We were wrong. Look over there!" They looked across the creek, now filled with water, and only bordered with its grass. Two miles on the farther side, on a patch of green land reclaimed from the heath, was a noble group of trees round a white farm.

"We should have gone there," said Felix—"this comes of Picus's swank about knowing the heath. This leads only to a place we called Misery, because they starved their dogs."

"I saw no tracks in the sand," said Carston.

"I supposed you knew the way." He heard them screaming like gulls over dead fish and would have preferred the birds' company. Abusing each other for what they would forgive in two minutes. Consider rather a joke.

Forget. They none of them saw that Picus had done it on purpose. Then Carston admitted that he might not have thought of it himself if the night before Picus had not slept with the woman he wanted. Why had he done it? He had separated himself from the woman, to mislead them.

They were lurching back through the sand the way they had come. But they had forgotten where they had entered the sunk road that led nowhere in particular; followed it as it wound into exactly the middle of everywhere, and looking over its bank found the airy roofs of Starn lost behind a line of high black trees.

Forgiveness woke in them and fatigue. Picus had been mocked for vanity, had mocked back, and set them off laughing. They were nervous, sweating, flushed. Felix shrieked when a snake flicked across his shoe. But it was all part of a game. Hardly able to see more than the sky, they trudged the road the sun had made into Danae's chimney, down which God came in a shower of gold. Clarence led them. Picus followed. He had deprecated Carston's suggestion that they should try and cut across the creek and make for the farm. "Bad bog," he said. "Marsh-king's sons," said Felix, "that would be the end of us," and Clarence that he had seen a pony lost there. At this choice of pleasures, Carston had followed them; and the sunk road, having come to the middle, stopped in a circular sand-bank round a foul pond bordered with marsh-grass where there was no way out. They flung themselves down.

It occurred to Carston that it was all nonsense. They had only a few miles to go. Keeping towards the long hills, they must strike a road and eventually, Starn. At Starn there was water, tea, lime-juice, gin, champagne. The liverish grass and thick water displeased him. "We can't stay for ever in this cup," he said.

Picus was asleep, Clarence bending over him. An odd sort of pietà. Felix was sinking in the mud, collecting a plant he said was for Ross. All careful of each other's needs and pleasures. He heard Clarence call softly: "Wet a hand-kerchief, Felix, I want it for his head." Saw it brought over, and Picus jump up in a flash. "None of that sort of water for me, thanks." To spite the men who took care of him? Probably. Carston felt that he was being given an opportunity to hate and that was good. "Hadn't you better try and get us out of this?" The tall creature looked at him, sadly. "I'll try; but you'll have to leave it to me again, you know." He sprang up the hollowed bank, kicking mouthfuls of sand into Carston's face, and vanished. Carston crawled up to watch, hiding behind the heather rim. He saw Picus run a few yards and fling himself down on his face. He waited and saw him get up, heard him call "It's this way," saw him glance round and make off. Carston called back to the other three, heaved himself over, and they set off on a slight track towards the belt of wood.

They went in. Pine-needles are not easy to walk on, like a floor of red glass. It is not cool under them, a black scented life, full of ants, who work furiously and make no sound. Something ached in Carston, a regret for the cool brilliance of the wood they had left, the other side of the hills, on the edge of the sea. This one was full of harp-noises from a wind when there was none outside. He saw Picus ahead, a shadow shifting between trunk and trunk. Some kind of woodcraft he supposed, and said so to Felix who said sleepily: "Somebody's blunt-faced bees, dipping under the thyme-spray"; a sentence which made things start living again. Would they never have enough of what they called life? There was no kind of a track over the split vegetable glass. A place that made you wonder what sort of nothing went on there, year in year out.

The end of the wood was a little cliff, pitted with rabbit holes; and where the hills opened, Starn towering, not too far.

"We get down here," said Carston, trying the loose lip of the cliff.

"Into what?" said Felix. Then they saw that the wood was surrounded again by marsh, the end of the creek which had separated them from Ross and Scylla, curled round on itself. Cutting them off from Starn this time. Clarence said: "Where's Picus?" and Carston hoped that young man was about to get what was coming to him. Only he had gone. They began to think of their sins. Except Carston, who did not think of sins at all. There was raw heath on the other side, but the marsh was wide, and Carston was assured deadly. They left the little cliff's edge, and re-entered the wood. He heard Felix saying: "Where has Picus gone?" Gone to find Scylla? Carston wondered. By a quick turn which would bring him suddenly face to face. And at the folly of three strong young men, tramping about, lost and sapped.

"Call for him," he said. "He'd not answer," said Clarence—"he may have had one of his bad pains again." Carston wished one on him, making an image of him in his anger, until he thought he saw him, walking towards them, transparent and powerful, malicious and shy; his hat perched, to remind them of hooded birds. Remembered his magic, and forgave him. Grew angry again and dazed. Envious also, because he had no part in Picus's dance. "Leave him alone," he said, "he's gone to find a way." Clarence put a hand on his shoulder; thanks, he supposed, for taking it like that.

At last, from the extreme end of the wood, in the least propitious place, they saw across the marsh a clear causeway of stone.

They scrambled down, crossed it, found a path which led them under the hills by a white road into Starn.

About the end of the walk, the less said the better, until at the inn the landlord answered their faint cries for drink. He wanted to know why they had left six and come back three.

"Lost 'em," said Felix.

"You should have stuck to Mr. Tracy. He's the one for the heath. Knows all the paths, and the people who bide out there."

The talk petered out. The evening marched gravely down. The two undoubtable shops put up shutters. The tourists had gone. A man came through with a bunch of sheep. The bar of the labourer's inn turned on a gramophone. From time to time, a huge man came in from the fields, making for his beer. The cries of children stopped. Mothers came out. A fast touring-car shot across the square. A mist rose, an intangible gauze, refreshing them. They dined in the inn garden. When Carston saw in the west a large star watching, he though of the lights on Broadway. Felix saluted the star. Clarence worried, but without, for once, worrying them.

They set out to watch the square again.

Then Scylla appeared, and Picus and Ross.

"We found him, sitting on a stone, saying he had lost you: that you ran away from him on Hangar's ridge."

"He lost you first," said Ross. "I don't blame you."

"He did," said Felix, "and cleared off when he'd made a final mess of it. I know his ways. Have you got the mead?"

"Bottles," said Scylla.

They were surprised when Picus, who had thrown himself into a chair, got up and said: "That's how you take it. It was not my fault."

Clarence sprang beside him.

As he went out, Scylla touched his sleeve with her fingers. He took no notice, but Clarence did.

Carston's fatigue had passed into charity. They were all over-tired, of course. The developments of over-fatigue were caprice and anger. What had Picus been up to? Helping himself with accidents, of course. But exasperating himself.

"There were no bones broken," he said, "you've got the mead, and we've all got back." He was furious when Clarence ignored him, and went out into the half-light after the man who seemed to combine all the elements of a family curse. Felix began:

"God! I'm sick of this. Why can't we be at Biarritz leading a reasonable life?"

A negro song came into Carston's head: *Bear your burden in the heat of the day:* but it did not occur to him to tell it to the boy, whom it would have helped.

Clarence came in again. "I've ordered the car. We ought to get back. I'll tell the others." Carston saw him go into the dining-room and heard Scylla call:

"Well, we want to eat. Tell it to wait."

"We must go home."

"Take it home then, and send it back for us."

Silence again. Question of expense.

Carston saw Picus come into the dining-room from the garden and sit down at a table by himself. He heard Scylla call:

"Clarence, leave your fancy-boy alone."

That had done it.

Picus was eating alone. Anything might happen, only it was time for sleep. Half an hour later they had packed into the car and shot away, up into the hills the night wind had now made exquisite, to a different wood from the one in whose red-glass darkness Picus had lost them, moist and shimmering, a repetition of the tremblings of the stars.

Chapter X

THE NEXT MORNING the sky was white round a blue zenith. Carston came down, not pleased, because through every discomfort of soul he was feeling well, his body content with itself, a steady animal health. He should have been all of a tremble, and he was hoping that there would be fish for breakfast, lots of fish. There was fish, and after it the toast came up, hot and hot. He remembered again to make opportunity serve him. Health would give him power. Also he would desire Scylla more. Desiring her more, and not wholly as panache he might get her. Picus was bound to let her down. He was saying: "I'm sorry I lost my temper. It was trying to lose you three like that. You know how one is." Scylla said:

"Served you right, when you'd lost them."

"How did you do it?" said Ross.

There was no answer. Picus was giving the impression that he was about to flirt his tail and vanish. Carston was irritated again. There came droning into his mind an ugly sentence, a haunting from barren New England: *Thou shalt not suffer a witch to live.* He was hearing Picus say: "How's the cup this morning?" and saw Scylla get up for it.

It was not on the card-table, folded over in a half-moon. It was not on the chimney-piece, or on the side-board among the candlesticks, whose silver had worn down to the copper and polished rose.

They passed the morning entering and leaving rooms where the cup was not. Not in the kitchen, the lavatory, or the library. In twos and threes and singly, getting more silent as they passed each other. Up and down the curved stairs whose banister was a rope run through rings. Carston saw a good deal in that journey. Scylla's room which had its objects of luxury, where the first time he stared at the bed, he suffered and desired to throw himself on to it. In and out of the room several times, he became indifferent, content with repeating to himself: "I shall sleep there." Picus's room, non-committal, in exquisite order like a manly woman's and Clarence's, full of frivolities. Then he remembered something he had read about an Emperor's collection of hats and wigs 'which sometimes solace the leisure of a military man.' There were no wigs and no hats. But no memory in that place ever had a straight point. Only his room was a sad, gay, desperate display of something like toys. He pitied, without humour, having no humour; slightly wanting for himself a glass orange, each of whose fingers came out and held a different kind of scent.

All their things for art or sport were cared for like tools or choice animals. In Felix's room there were leopard skins; in Ross's a Buddha in a red lacquer shrine held a crystal, a reflection for their mutual contempt.

And the beds were humble and the linen darned, the bare floors solid like glass rocks. He could feel the weight of the blue slate roof, cooling and darkening the rooms, holding the house to the earth, while they searched it like serious children for a thing which could not walk. In and out and up and down a house much larger than it seemed, cooler than the wood's heart.

Dazed Carston played too, arrived at the long attic, roaring dark, directly under the roof. The roar was from bees who hived under the slates, and the smell their fresh honey and the black clots, old combs. There was Felix opening a victorian work-box made out of an elephant's foot. A place where it was utterly impossible for the cup to be. No more impossible than that it should have been overlooked anywhere else. Short of idiocy, a miracle, or a trick, the thing was off the map. A conclusion they had reached by lunch-time, after a morning's exercise indoors.

It was a quiet meal. Two things had been lost. Picus

and a cup. Picus had found himself. As for the cup, they had reached the time before the time for real consideration, when the instinct is to find something else to do. Carston, no more than the others, was quite ready to say that, since six pairs of eyes had failed to see something, then that thing must have been hidden, and hidden well. Instead he was made unhappy, because he heard Picus say to Scylla: "We don't want to bathe to-day, do we? Come over to Gault Cliff and I'll shew you something—"

"Birds?" He nodded once. "I'm coming."

They were in the library, the sacred neutral zone for arrangements that had no reference to their life as a group. An arrangement Carston could not be expected to have understood. It was a very dark room. From a window seat he saw their bodies straining to be away. And hated it. Like a man put in a bag and shaken up, instincts were stirring in him, like muscles unused in years, and sore and strengthening.

The american appears to the english everything that is implied by saying over-sensitive, touchy, or abnormally quick to take offence. Our reaction is usually bewilderment, grief that our intentions have been misunderstood. Followed by a desire to give them something to cry about.

Carston thought they had seen him, could not have understood that no one was seen in that room. And they had not seen him. If they had, they would have supposed that he was there not to be seen. Scylla was sitting on the top of the library steps, made like everything in the house before the days of cheap furniture, shabby and characteristic as an old dog. She said to Picus:

"You idle baggage, what have you found on the hills?"

"Come and see!"

"Let me down!" He put his hands under her arm-pits and let her down, so gently that Carston did not hear her feet touch the floor. He saw their colours; her white; Picus's blue and grey. He saw their beauty, their own, and the beauty of their passion. And another thing; that the man's right hand ought not to belong to his body; that it was red and thick and swollen at the joints. He remembered the delicate adaptability of Ross's, Felix's, Clarence's hands. This gave him a key. To a very old feeling about sin and fleshy lust. A refinement on sensuality, he knew, but an excuse for rage. And a warm feeling that what would relieve him would be right. Right for him to possess Scylla, if he had first rescued her. That would give him the claim on her body. Rescue her from what? From passion for a tall delicate man with coarse hands. Also because he had glory, a kind of lost god. From what was the glory? From the devil. How did one shame the devil? By taking the honour out of his sufferings. *Thou shalt not suffer a witch to live.* And the reward would be Scylla.

What would he give her? Respect, for he did not respect her, or at least admire. Sincerity, loyalty, virility— after what? He was sure Picus did not respect her, was not sincere with her, had no loyalty, and he didn't know about the last. The fantasy in this sequence escaped him, because of the naïveté of his cult for women. He had made a martyr of a person who was not a martyr, or to nothing which would have moved him. In the world there is a fifty-fifty deal of pleasure and grief. The excuse of that band was that they knew it, and that they had something else to occupy their attention, something that the wood knew.

When they had gone, Carston went to the wall where a map hung, to look for a place called Gault Cliff. As well to know where they were going. He followed the coast with his thumb, and found it. About three miles away. There was a track they would probably take; and a way where no track was marked over God knew what to God knew where, which might get him there before them.

The others seemed to expect him to want to be left very much alone. Praise their country and give them the slip? Or take Felix down to the sea and make him talk?

He decided to do that.

Chapter XI

Picus and scylla went out of the house along the green road, walking separately. They sprang up the hill, the air from the sea fortifying them, against the mid-day, against the desire to anticipate in thought a distance their muscles must cover.

They came to the coast where Ross had sat and painted, his back to the house. "This way," said Picus, and turned through a gate into a tunnel of hawthorns where a bird had flown out before Ross. There Scylla paused, but he took no notice, and she fell behind him, following his stride.

The way became hard, no way at all, but climb and drop over unmortared stone walls, bound with bramble and thorn. They crossed them, without reference to each other, steady as hunting dogs. In time they came to the edge of Gault.

"Let's go down!"

"How?"

"On the soft side, where the landslide was last winter. Can you do it?"

"I suppose so." She looked where a coast-path ran to the edge, straight out into mid-air.

Some time later they were in the unvisited wood under Gault, where the low trees grow to the edge of the sea. Where there is no bay, no beach, no landing-place, no way round. Taking advantage of a great fall of earth, Picus had created a way down.

From the immense crag water dripped, and ran out under the roots of a thorn over the tidemark of the open sea. They followed it up to where it ran over pebbles across a circle of grass enclosed by low trees. Greenwood within whispering distance of the unharvested sea. She said:

"What have you found here?"

"What d'you mean?"

"The way down—and this—"

"Foxes, badgers, fifteen ways of looking at a finch. They don't mind you here."

High over them the gulls squalled like sorrow driven up. At long intervals the water tapped the rocks like memory driven away. She knelt over the stream and washed dust and clay and a smear of blood from her bare arms and neck. Pulled a trail of thorns from her skirt. Threw away her hat.

"This is Bari," she said, "the warm wood."

"Which one was that?" said Picus, off his guard.

"Baldur's wood," she said, very carefully, not to make a mistake with him.

Gault Cliff hung over them, a terror to look up at, its seamed head raw in the light, but dark underneath and broken into bog and scree, interlude between the earth of pure stone, and the earth of wood and spring. No interval between the wood and the sea, it was that made the place incomparable. They lay on the grass on each side of the foot-wide brook, paddling their hands.

"Not bad for a naked sword," she said. He kissed her over it. "Hush!" A bird appeared. She cried out: "That's a Great Black Woodpecker."

"I've been looking for it all my life," he said. "Chuck!" said the bird at them and went off. They saw the scarlet ribbon on its head.

"What else is there here?"

"There's a badger that bit me, and a vixen I can almost nurse—there's the skeleton of a man—"

"We won't look there now—"

"Not to-day, love." She crossed her hands on her breast. He had given her all he had. This place. A fountain where saga and love were mixed. She looked up into the sky at Gault Cliff, where the mica glittered like sweat.

Again Picus said: "Hush!" She listened, loving him. The bird was back, the largest and rarest of the woodpeckers.

"I saw him when I was looking at the skeleton. In a tree."

She said: "He was a famous bird once, Picus Martius. He was Zeus." He nodded, as if he was saying: "I thought as much." But she had turned the corner where love sees. When she saw that she was lying by the same thing. That what she had said to confuse them prettily, to hide love by revealing, had been about this. Between the tree and the skeleton there had been the bird who had been god. He had seen it, who was called Picus the Woodpecker, who was a man, who was the same thing. Now she knew, who was her lover. And what was she now, the lover of a bird?

Even Leda found a blue egg. She laughed. How long was this going to last? What was this? It was all right; worth whatever it hatched.

Only he must make love to her there.

He had rolled up the sleeves of his blue sweater. He put out his arms, one marked with a badger-bite, across the stream and slung her over.

It was late afternoon. They were lying again on either side of the stream. Gault over them, a little blacker with the sun turning behind it.

"How did you come to find this place?"

"Last spring, looking for young gulls. I looked down and thought if I found a lover—"

"Any lover?"

"I have only found one."

She kissed him over the ribbon of water. He said:

"There's a nest in every crack of the rock. It's still pretty full." That took away her fear of Gault. For the terrible crag was soft with birds, and where the birds ended the spring rose. None of the sequence without grace.

They were coming out of the trance of love into a time which would have to be put up with until luck turned them birds again. He had given her his treasure. If he rose and strangled her, she had that to remember to him. There was trouble in his face, the old trouble, Picus's grief. That was not named or rational or tamed or shared. Untractable, inexplicable, near to wickedness.

The water divided them. She crossed it. He moved his hands as though he would be rid of them.

"Shew me the skeleton!" He shook his head.

"Make the bird come back! I want to see him again."

"Woodpecker-Zeus," she said, "leave your skeleton under the tree. Stop flirting with us. We know who you are. Eagle. Kingfisher. Swan. We have met you before. I am Leda. You know best who he is."

She waited, hoping for the best.

"There it is," said Picus. She could not see it. The shadow of the cliff was moving towards them.

"In the thicket." She clapped her hands, and the bird flew out.

"There," she said, and saw him suddenly pleased and changed.

Then he said:

"Wonder what that chap Carston'll make of it?"

"Make of what?"

They were looking at the other out of the corner of their eyes. Picus paddled one hand in the stream.

Scylla said:

"There is one thing which may have surprised him already. His room's between ours."

"Well, that ought to interest him."

"Only," she said, "if he wanted me."

"He may be wanting you. Perhaps you'd better sleep with him. It would be better than his coming down here. Where nothing has been spoiled, love."

"I see. Mais comme tu taquines éternité."

She thought again: 'I have no business to be glad that

Clarence does not know, nor ask if he will be taken here.
I came first.' This was an excuse, not only in honour, but
in letting life alone.

He got up and drew her on to her feet. He walked her
along the grass between the thickets and boulders, so that
her feet never touched a stone. Up the landslide she
hardly felt the slant of the earth, held as if he were walking
with a tree. At the top of the cliffs he gave her no time to
look back. In their triumph they walked alone a little separate from each other.

At a gate he caught her up.

"What y' thinking about?" She saw his head on one
side.

"Carston and the cup. That ought to get him going
more than us."

"Perhaps it will."

"Picus, demon, where did you hide it?"

"Hush! love."

Chapter XII

AFTER AN ACCIDENT in the sea with a small octopus he would sooner have avoided, Carston returned to the house. Felix had not talked to him, said that it would be wiser not to talk, because there might be big magic about. Could not Carston feel it cooking up? Convinced that the boy was enjoying himself, he went up to his room. And what was there to do but think of those two, up somewhere high in air, kissing, or finding some strangeness in Nature and forgetting to kiss. He lay staring and fretting, until with slow alarm growing like a dream, he saw the lost cup, by itself, on the end of his mantelpiece. And earlier in the day, they had passed in and out of his room looking for it there.

His first impulse was to run downstairs with it, crying. Crossing the room to take it, he slipped on the glassy boards, and the fall and anger from pain turned him. He did not want to touch it. There might be something about it after all. Working a splinter out of his hand, it occurred to him that they had put it there; that the morning had been a farce played for his benefit, a vile joke to make a fool of him. Those people who made love under his eyes, who had lost him on a moor. They had not let him into their lives. They would not believe his innocence. Under the shock of his fall, his imagination galloped reeling. He felt very lonely. He was very lonely. It did not cross his head that they would believe what he told them. Still less that it did not matter whether they believed him or not. Behind this, a dead fever reviving in the blood, was the literal fear of the cup, that it was uncanny, tabu. He passed a dreadful minute, staring at its impressive antiquity. His sensitive intelligence raced through a variety of panics, till the shock of his fall subsided and he began to arrange alternatives. To go down to tea with the cup and say: "I found it in my room. I don't know how it got there."

To hide it in his baggage. In the house. To put it somewhere—say, in Picus's room. To destroy it.

The first would make a fool of him, the second a thief, the third impossible, the fourth a trickster; the fifth might bring bring him to a bad end. This was what had come of his nosing round for power. Scylla would be coming in, burnt with kisses. Perhaps she had played off this trick on him. How many years had he been living in this chinese box of tricks? If he could have believed in their belief of the possibility of a possible sanctity, gone down to them and said: "Here is something that may be precious," he would have walked into their hearts. But that would not have served him, because he did not want their hearts. Did not want hearts. Wanted scalps.

On a final sweep of rage he went downstairs with a cup in his hands to Felix and Clarence and Ross. He said: "Here's your cup. I should like to know which of you played this off on me. I should like to know who put it in my room."

"Oopsey daisy," said Felix.

"If that's your notion of hospitality, it doesn't coincide with mine."

Clarence said: "If you don't like us, what d'you come down here for?"

"What we mean, is," said Ross, "that we don't understand why you should think such a thing."

"Are you trying it out on me that the thing got there by itself, and that none of you knew?" Felix said:

"If we had known, why should we have spent a morning perspiring over it?"

Carston cried at him:

"I'd not put it past you. The day I turn my back on you

all will be the best I've spent. I can tell people then what I think of you."

Felix answered: "And we might as well tell the world that your thirst for antiquities led you to steal a family chalice. Nice kind of mind you've got. You know none of us put it in your room." That was what he did not know. What he could not have done, others could do. There was a stupid, broken pause. Then he said, who had had time to think:

"I suppose the alliance between Miss Taverner and Mr. Tracy explains it."

"What alliance explains what?"

Carston looked at the brother; felt like a man pulling up blinds.

"Love made them mischievous, I suppose."

"What love?"

Warm, sunburnt, they came in. They were in the room, leaning on their ashplants, serene, apart. After a silence, "What's wrong?" said Scylla.

"The cup's turned up," said Ross, "in Carston's bedroom. Did either of you put it there?"

Knowing Picus behind her, she laughed. Lovers' jokes are sacred, pleasantries of a man who discovers the seawood, the rock soft with birds, the meeting of pure water and salt. Come down out of that to enchant and rule her equals.

"Count us out," she said. "What's biting you, Carston?"

If she had shewn a little decent concern it might have recalled him. But he went on:

"Then I suppose your friend did it. Not content with keeping me awake all night."

They stared at him. Clarence was practically invisible with frightful emotion.

"Put what where?" said Picus, laughing.

"Four mysteries," said Carston, "since I got here. First, you found that thing. Then Tracy vanished, after leading us a dance in an infernal prairie. Then the thing vanished. Then it's found in my room. I'm waiting your explanations. I've gotten my own."

"Let's hear 'em," said Ross.

Scylla spoke: "It is my cup. My lover who gave it me. We who have enjoyed it. Carston can think what he likes. I did not put it in his room. It is he who will not play. If he wants to find out what has happened, he will find out. We will tell him when we know. Which we don't at present. Don't be a fool, man. No one has tried to trick you here."

All fairly true, but Picus had done something. Just a little devilry. Her heart caught at a beat, she tasted something in her mouth, salt like pain. Pain so soon after. Other side of the halfpenny. She sneered and sat down, tapping the bright boards with her stick.

Carston felt disintegrating, sticky, a loser, afraid. Still standing, he stared out at the wood, at the ilex-limb, each leaf a white-fire flame. He became aware of all the noises of the wood, that it was cackling all the time, a frightful old long gossip about dirt and the dead ends of lies. His subtle brain raced on, took a glorious chance. He said:

"I can tell you something then. Tracy has a book up in his room. On somebody's collection of early church ornaments. He brought the cup down from London to work this off on you all. You remember how he stunted his ignorance? Just a little game to make you think something of yourselves and let you down. You may like being kidded. I don't. I reckon I've done you a service—"

"Bright idea," said Felix. "True, Picus?" He flew at them, with the menaces of a bird.

"What d'you mean? Scylla's been talking. You are all a pack of old women intriguing against me. Making my life hell. Like Carston, I'm sick of your hospitality. Especially when it includes him."

"*Our hospitality*," said Felix. Quotation wasted on Picus, caught Carston.

"Yes, a decent vendetta would be better than your poisoned fun."

"We don't seem to have cleaned up anything," said Clarence.

"Cleaned up," said Picus, chattering at them. "Accusing me. Boring me. Interfering with ME." In this there was something that was not comic, in the dis-ease he imparted.

"An aborted thunderstorm," said Scylla. "I'm going up to change."

Five left, hating each other. Then Felix modestly, like the youngest: "I'll go down the wood, and see about the dinner fish." Four left. "Work to do," said Ross. Three left. "Have you a time table?" said Carston. Clarence said: "Hadn't you better stay till we know the truth?" Carston turned his back on him, and went out neatly through the library door. Two left.

"What is this about you and Scylla?"

"I suppose I am free to sleep with whom I like?"

"Why her?"

"Why not? You don't want her."

"God, no. But you might have told me."

"I thought I heard her tell you."

"So you and Scylla are one voice then?"

Picus laughed again. "She shouldn't have told." Clarence smiled back at him faintly, as if he had to smile under pain, his own, anyone's. And Picus chattered on, all of him dancing together, subtle, venomous, absurd.

Clarence listened, till the time came when he could listen no longer, and hid his face, the awful pain rising in him, drowning Picus's presence. And he was thankful for it. Escape into infinite suffering, a deadly grey land, and he was thankful for it. Away from Picus for ever. Not even to meet the true Picus, but to the country where there was no Picus. When that had gone away for ever. That nerve dead. *Free among the dead.* He raced away on that black heath. Of course, the place where Picus had lost them the day before. But that country had been sapphire and purple, wild with bees. He was out there now in December.

> *The North cannot undo them.*
> *With a sleepy whistle through them.*

True for trees, but what about the 'gentle girl and boy'? He had hidden himself a long time in the pain.

When he took his hands away from his face, Picus had gone.

Chapter XIII

SCYLLA WENT UPSTAIRS, and lying on her bed in her shift felt her elation and clean fatigue replaced by shabby weariness and fear.

Picus had played that trick on Carston. Picus had spoiled her pride in him. Why had he played a spiteful joke? She had not begun to think it possible that he had arranged the story of the cup. Only the trick on Carston was ill-mannered, a little cruel. Also irrelevant. It had made the business seem empty, like the effect got at séances where the interesting, the decisive, the clear is always on the point of arrival, and invariably fades out before the point is reached.

Like the mass of keltic art. Like, now she considered it, the whole Grail story, the saga story *par excellence* that has never come off, or found its form or its poet. Not like the Golden Fleece or Odysseus at Circe's house. There was something in their lives spoiled and inconclusive like the Grail story. It would be her turn next for Picus to insult, as he had played a pointless joke on a foreign guest. A number of unpleasant emotions followed that thought, chiefly disturbed sexual vanity which sets the earth by the ears. Life was ice-bright, and disagreeable as flint. It was a maudlin dream. Chance couplings, little minds setting to partners. Victory of ants over the sphinx in flesh: over birds.

She watched the flies flashing across the window, a bee searching a flower head in a jar of mixed wild stalks Felix had put there. Then to detach herself she played an old game, that she was lying out on the wood's roof: translating the stick and leaf that upheld her into herself: into sea: into sky. Sky back again into wood, flesh and sea.

It did not work, as it was meant to, to deliver her from herself, but it made her see Picus's proceedings diabolic. Why so? Parody of a mystery. A mystery none of them believed. That reduced it to a bad taste. They did not quite disbelieve. Dangerous fooling then? Parodied also in her bed. Very cruel and so wrong.

But under Gault Cliff there had been no parody. That she had to love Picus by, as much of a creation as any growth in nature. Or ritual, or rite produced by the imagination. As little symbolic as the result of any mystery propitiously performed.

As she attended to what she was thinking, she laughed, her immense vitality racing back. Her entry had made his trick glorious. Dinner would be difficult. What had been wrong with Carston? She would go and talk to him. What about? She would propitiate Felix. How? They will all hate me. Without whom Picus would not have turned creator. Woman's place indeed. Clarence wanted that job. He did the work, and I wear the crown. Not my fault. Chances of the sacred game.

Swept off into stadium of the game; which is the pleasure in actions for their own sake. Done for the love of playing. Done for the fun of it. Done for no pompous end.

That Felix was just a little nervous about.

Played by Alexander, and young Cleopatra in a bundle at Caesar's feet.

Played by that demon Picus, when he had whistled up mystery with what was now undoubtedly a victorian finger-bowl.

Played by Malatesta having Isotta sculped for the Madonna; and the man who broke the bank at Monte Carlo.

Played by Chaucer who loved everything for what it was. A sword for being a sword, or a horse. And they for what they were, the 'gentle girls and boys.'

Good thinking, good eating. All things taking care of themselves. Each thing *accordynge to its kynde*.

Would there be a train for Carston to go away by? Good idea of Picus to say it would be better for him to be slept with than visit that wood.

Was there anything to eat for dinner, anyhow? She jumped up and went out discreetly through the kitchen. In the scullery there was Felix, cleaning a basket of fish. Too much fish. Enough for half to go bad, and the rest infuriate Picus, who would say he had been given it to encourage his brain. Felix said:

"I thought I might as well help. Nanna and Janet are at it all day. Nothing like getting in a stock. Had a good walk with Picus?"

The basket, full of fish-shapes, was wet, black-ribboned inside, a shell sticking here and there, a live whelk walking up. Sea-smelling, almost living food, still running with the live sea. She took a knife and a fish, and cut down on the slab of dark blue slate used for cooling butter. Felix had covered it with scales and blood.

"We'll do it together," she said.

"You're not very good at it," he said.

She hesitated, testing the contact with him.

"We'll do other things together, then."

"Don't we pretty well always?" —His knife scraped down on a bone— "I mean, it's only half the time I don't understand."

She thought: 'So he went and gutted fish for me.' She said: "What, my dearest dear, did you understand to-day?" He answered: "When you came in with Picus I saw your beauty. After Carston had been talking, and surprised me, rather. After the things which have happened lately. It was a kind of answer. A sudden opposite to what I was thinking. To what the world is usually, I suppose. You see, I would sooner have you or even Picus in the right. Only, I haven't faith."

She thought: 'Try and have faith. No. Don't try and have anything. Be with me.'

And in answer, she told him about the wood. The bird, Picus. *O lady, be good.* Everything. That she could not have told the others. She heard a thought in his head: 'I shan't be able to keep this up, but to-day I am my sister's.'

More love for her now, handed back through Carston's spite; peace in the scullery with her flesh and blood. Fish blood and flesh on a stone between them. In one day, two kinds of perfect love. Life with Picus. Life with him. (He had understood love for Picus. Picus would not understand love for him.) Life without Picus? Life without him? She remade Antigone's discovery that you can have more lovers and more children. Not another brother, once your people's bearing days are gone.

Life with the two gone. Life with Clarence, Carston, Ross? She thought she heard a voice saying: "You will soon be left alone with them. You will be without Felix. Because there is coming to you the opposite of what you've had. Must come to you. More than separation; avoidance, treachery. Equal to what you've had. At one point, life without them will mean that."

"Not if I can help it!"

Behind this somewhere was an immense discovery, a huge principle which made it immaterial if she could help it or not. She rested in the knowledge that it was there. Their nurse came in, and they thought at once of washing and going away to change. Mounting the stairs, their arms round each other's shoulders, Carston saw them from his room, and was inexpressibly shocked, unable to understand how Scylla had persuaded her brother that her relations with Picus had been misunderstood.

Chapter XIV

As FELIX SAID, "pep" had been the *mot juste* for the way Carston behaved. When he had found that there was no train that night, he had walked across the valley. There he had discovered a coast-guard, and, practically unaided, the system by which the station wireless picked up the lighthouse, and from there communicated by telegraph with Starn. From this, he produced a taxi and a lodging for the night. He walked back and packed vigorously, kneeling on the floor, his back to the window and the wood. When he had seen Scylla passing upstairs with her brother, he had shut his door, ceased to hear the silence of the house, heard instead the wood, a little restless, its branches changing places in a wind risen suddenly off the sea.

Odd that he would not see the place again; have no part with its men, or possess its woman. Never found out what had really happened.

He was still on the crest of the energy he had spent in denouncing them in a general sensation of burned boats. There had not risen yet doubt of himself, scrutiny, not of his motives, he knew better than to do that, but of the figure he had cut. Yet, his angry elation was like a fir-cone fire, needing baskets of brittle wood-shells. He had a fine story for his friends, something to think about. Scylla written off as a bad job, as a romance. It seemed equally impossible to say good-bye, to leave without saying it. Then the old nurse knocked, told him that his taxi was there, and that Mr. Felix, Miss Scylla, and Mr. Ross wished him a pleasant journey. He tipped her enormously, slipped across the verandah, fearing heads that were not watching. With jars and jerks, the taxi crept up the long hill.

Divine escape. On the down-crest, the earth was a map of naked beauty he saw in the piece and understood. "I've been living inside a work of art"—living what was meant to be looked at, not lived in; not to be chewed, swallowed, handled, kissed. He lay back, rocking over the grass track, almost satisfied with this. A piece of life, definitely over for him, with the stone age, and the Middle Ages, and— A patch of purple gauze ahead, smoke of no earthly fire, now a patch of those tall, bee-shaken spikes they called foxgloves. As they passed it, he saw thin legs stuck out of it along the earth, a body backed against the flower wall. It was Picus out there, up there. Looking out at nothing; out to sea. Sitting on the top of the world.

Chapter XV

AT STARN he was refreshed again with contacts from outside. There was an unusual number of tourists, two and two on the hillpaths, swarming the square. They did him so much good that he crossed to the station to meet a down-train that held more. Not many get out at evening, where there was nothing to do but stare. All he noticed in particular was an old gentleman.

He was beginning to enjoy the country. Enjoy Starn. Would have liked to know more, its history and contemporary life. He thought the old man with a red face, in grey flannels, a local landowner; thought him back to some dignified house, and was surprised later to see him dining at the inn.

He was not known there, it seemed. There was a difficulty about a room for him. Carston felt that he should leave graciously, suggested that the old man should have his room, and he a bed anywhere. There was consultation, hesitation, acceptance, thanks. After an interval, they had settled down to coffee together.

It was easy to be charming to him. An obvious number of right things to say. In a flash that, too, had passed.

"So you've been staying over at Gault House with the Taverners. Did you meet my son there—Picus, I think they call him? My name's Tracy."

Carston thought: 'Be cautious, be very cautious indeed. Don't tell lies. The old man will be going there. His eyes are the colour of his flannels. What we call stone, and never is. Stone takes light.'

"Yes," he said, "he is staying there with his friends."

It became suddenly necessary to observe with every faculty he had. He had no idea why; not for distraction, not with reference to himself. The impression was that he was opposite someone very old—not particularly in years, but in something built by centuries of experience, and now no longer in flower. The same could be said of his son and his son's friends, only that they were in flower, and might not cease flowering once their bodies' bloom was done. Centuries had gone to his construction. Carston was surprised at his attention to this, until he noticed that their setting outside the inn was the setting of a play.

Before he had wished for drama, and had not found his rôle. Now he was too much of a man to take himself off.

The stage surpassed all romantic expectations, a town with towers, in hills high enough and low enough to set and display it equally. A fleece of stars over it, thick as the flocks on the down-sides, turning, turning with the earth.

"Do you like this country?" the old man said.

"I like it immensely. I am sorry to leave. I only came down for the week-end."

"Still, you prolonged it. This is Friday."

Carston thought: 'A nice slip to start off with. I'd better be a bit more frank right away.' "To tell you the truth, I'm a stranger, and I found things a bit difficult over there."

"Would it surprise you to hear that I've heard that said before?"

"Not at all."

They laughed together. Carston began to think backwards. The eighteenth century had produced this type, had set him in culture and conviction that Nature had appointed certain old men to approve and modestly direct her arrangements of air and fire. The Renaissance had kicked off that ball, now frozen into the marble and stucco that he was sure adorned his park somewhere. Behind that there was the matrix; the Middle Ages, feudalism, Christendom. Faith in a childishly planned universe as one thing. *The earth one great city of gods and men.* His history lessons were taking life at last.

"I detest impertinence," the old man said—"I don't

think it will be necessary to go into that; but other people have found my son difficult. Was it anything to do with him?"

Carston thought: 'Picus again. In for some more. No good pretending.' He said:

"I reckon. Perhaps I didn't catch on—that he was fooling me."

'Like talking to an old stone idol; live stone idol; stone idol that walks: after something. I ate their bread, and I was rude to them. Be careful, be very careful, indeed. . . . '

"People, I hear, have left the house before, after what I could only wish was my son's sense of humour had come into play."

Carston saw that it was a question which was going to lure the other on. And he longed to tell someone something.

"Who are down there now?"

He gave the names. No harm in that.

The old man meditated: "Ah! the heart of the band?"

Why a band? More news.

"My son has a bad habit. He is fond of other people's property which may never be his. In this instance I am speaking for myself. He has a book of mine that I want. Also, it interests me to know why he should want it. And I may say that your quarrel interests me, whatever it was."

"Don't call it a quarrel. I just didn't like his way of going about things."

"And the rest of my family? We are all more or less related."

"I was to blame in part. Lost my temper and said more than I should, and they let me go."

"Very characteristic; of England, I mean. I am sorry. I suppose, by the way, you didn't see about the house a book on early Church vessels? If you had, it would be easier for me to call my son to order."

'Say no; say no; say no. A fool I shall look. He's seen I hesitated. What in hell does it matter?'

"I sort of remember a book like that in the library."

"Not in my son's room?"

"No, I was never there."

The old man did not seem pleasant; silent after he had been told a lie. Then he began to speak fast.

"As you have acknowledged a difficulty, I feel that I might as well tell you why I have come down—at least to find out whether that book is there or not. Why should he want it? He's quite illiterate. Only if he has it, I shall be on the track of what may be cropping up again. You know what I mean—romantic ideas, now that we know they are lies, which are liable to fall into very silly and very evil practices. Excuses for perversions."

Carston thought: 'It's coming out. The old man has a drink in him. *In vino veritas:* good old Montparnasse.' Again his curiosity, he said:

"There was nothing like that down there."

The old man said: "My book's gone—and if he has taken that he may have taken something else. There's his cousin, Scylla, there—"

"She is beautiful—"

"I am glad to hear she is up to your new-world standards. But an affair with her mixed up with superstition and theft."

"What is superstition over here?"

"A disgusting relic of non-understood natural law."

"I'm at sea."

"Of course, you are, and I'm glad to hear it, and that you saw nothing objectionable. In spite of your little difficulty, whatever it was."

"Tell me," said Carston, "what do you expect me to have seen?"

The old man considered: "A strained, shall we say, morbid situation between my son and Scylla Taverner. Repetition in another key with Clarence Lake. Remember, the idea of the first comes from you. The latter, I have frequently observed with disgust. So long as there has been no mention of a cup—"

'Cup. My God! And I'm half in mine.' Carston heard a noise like bells he distinguished for the blood in his ears. Then there rang over Starn a variation on three notes, flood-tide pouring into the hill circle, passing out down the valleys, striking and hushed at once on the grass cloth of the hills.

"Don't tell," said Starn bells. "Don't tell. Don't tell!"

He thought: 'I must tell something, I need to. There must be something I can tell. Not tell on them.'

The old man was talking with something in his voice of a stallion's scream:

"My son's after Scylla Taverner with a piece out of my collection. As if I didn't know where I got it, and all about it. And what put him up to it? And what'll that neurotic hussy make of it? But if he did it, I've got a surprise for them. Its story'll be the surprise, if he doesn't mind being turned out with his fancy girl—"

Not tell on them.

Carston said: "It isn't what you think, at all, Mr. Tracy. I've nothing against your son in general. I reckon now that I was jealous. You see, I'm in love with Miss Taverner, and his easy ways angered me. That's why I left."

At once he ceased to be an object of interest. But he was believed. Fooled the old man who was down there, up to less good than anyone else. The bells stopped. There was a feeling that the air had been emptied for ever. A cow mooed. Life started again. He went on easily:

"Funny how a love you feel is hopeless spoils your judgment. Goodness knows I never noticed anything of what you suggest. I just couldn't get inside their life, and I wanted to get into hers—"

"There was that book in the library," said the old man.

Inspiration came lightly.

"You half talked me into that. Now I remember it had

a book-plate in it, Felix Taverner's." 'If I fool him too much, he'll go to bed. And I ought to warn them. Warn them of what? That the old man knows the cup's gone. Certainly. Picus is the sort to take it out on Scylla. The Sanc-Grail theory's bust anyhow. Tell 'em that.' He listened to a theory of the rights of owners to their property which sounded exaggerated even in the mouth of an elderly english collector.

The old red lips moved unpleasantly in their thatch of dead-white hair:

Prupperty: prupperty: prupperty.

The earth one great city of gods and men.

He began to live again in moments of insight. They were exceedingly unlike the flashes by which they are generally described, more like obstructions removed, revealing a landscape that had always been there.

The old man seemed to have come out of the Roman world. That was difficult to understand, except on a theory that times are grouped otherwise than in sequences. What had his kind been doing at the time of the Roman world? When they had been pouring out of Britain, who had been pouring in? The ancestors of the peasants Carston had seen; but it was not a question of ancestors. There had been a story then of a king, a *comitatus* called Arthur, whose business had been divided between chasing barbarians and looking for a cup. A kind of intermezzo in history, in a time called the Dark Ages, which had produced a story about starlight. Suns of centuries had succeeded it, while the story had lived obscurely in some second-rate literature, and more obscurely, and as an unknown quality, in the imaginations of men like Picus and Scylla, Felix, Clarence, Ross. A very bad old man was putting an unpleasant finger into that pie. Carston was sure of one thing, that he disliked him more than his son. The old man was studying him, with coldness fired by brandy.

"I can't exactly promise to avenge your wrongs, Mr. Carston. But I assure you my son will regret it if he has tampered with my collection. If he has with him a small jade cup, quite ageless in appearance, and slightly ornamented, and if he has persuaded himself that it has some superstitious history, my visit may afford you some satisfaction."

Carston thought: 'He is mad about property, and he hates his son. And his son's lover, and youth and imagination, and all there is to love over there. He believes in something too. In the thing which he accuses in his son. Whatever that is. Something I can no more imagine in Picus than that Picus doesn't wash. The devils believe backwards. I can't grudge the man a trick or two with that behind him. Now I know the father, I can't hate the son any more.'

He noticed the bad moral that if he had stayed over there and behaved himself, he would not have had this interesting insight into his late hosts' private lives. Another brandy went down. He wanted to go for the old man on their behalf, and excited with drink he needed to talk. So long as he did not say the word *cup*.

"I assure you, sir, you won't find anything a father would object to in that house." 'He knows why I am saying this, because I've seen him.'

"They strike me as people who have loved and suffered a great deal. That purifies."

"From what?"

"From being like what you say— From only thinking of yourself." It is not agreeable to be dismissed like a baby. He had to remember that the old man hadn't seen through him.

"If you were to ask me, I should say that they were looking for something. Miss Taverner told me one day that what they wanted had been lost out of the world."

"When and what?" said the old man.

"I don't quite get their dates. Might have been any time, the Middle Ages, or the day before yesterday—a thing that's been lost—"

"There was only one thing lost of a symbolic value in the Middle Ages," said the old man.

Then Carston's cups influenced him to obvious caution—then to dreams. He saw Picus making pretty things, Felix laughing, Ross painting, Clarence sleeping, Scylla running away into thunder over burnt grass: running in, in love, through a rain wall.

The energy that had got him away must get him back, and damned early. He arranged to be called, arranged for a car, without question that the morning would find him in the same mind.

Chapter XVI

NEXT MORNING Carston was by no means in the same mind, and hardly in the same body. It occurred to him, as he looked out on to a village square full of bellying sea fog, that sleeping above him was an impeccable old gentleman of considerable resource and command, tracing a son who had robbed him. At the same time that the old man would be making an early start, or might be watching him from his sleep. That in going back he would be taking sides in a peculiarly unpleasant family row. If there had been a train before mid-day, he would have taken it. Instead, he took exaggerated precautions, sure of only one thing that he did not want to meet the old man again: told the boots he was driving to a farther village to see the church: hoped he bribed the driver of the car to silence.

Not until he was on the down-track again, by the fox-glove patch, did any of last night's elation return. He yielded to the idea that he was on a pilgrimage, dismissed the car, left his suit-case under a wall and walked the last mile. Over dew, through gauze and long sun-shafts down to the house.

Seven-thirty o'clock. The old nurse in an older dressing-gown was waking up the kitchen life. He asked for Scylla, the easiest and the hardest person to see, and waited for her below. She came down, heavenly sleepy. He told her that he was sorry, and what had happened at Starn.

"That's all right," she said, "everyone gets worked at times. I only wish you had not sprung it on Clarence—I'd like you to be sorry for that—no, *not* because it was bad manners but because it was cruel and damned silly—"

That punished him, though he did not understand her aversion to cruelty, that kind. She went on—"But a worse thing has happened, it may be for the best. It usually is—" Suddenly, the complications of the story came over her, and he heard a sort of cry: "What is it all about— I don't like this," and he saw that he meant to stay if he had to sleep out on the earth and gnaw grass to help her. Then she told him to go down and bathe before breakfast, while she told the rest, and gave his case to the old nurse.

"Take it up to Mr. Carston's room. He did good work for us last night at Starn."

A little breakfast with the Borgia's. Poison anyhow, hurrying up over the hills. No woodpecker, no appetites. Clarence handing back with interest his insolence of the day before.

Scylla said:

"Clarence, we must be practical. Go and find out what Picus has tried to do." And Carston could have kicked the man when he assured her that it was now her business.

"It's not become that," she answered, steadily—"go you and manage him, as you have always done."

No, Clarence would not. Waited to be entreated to have more fun in refusing.

"Are we going to lie, or aren't we?" said Felix.

"That depends on Picus." It did.

"Whatever we do, he'll do the opposite." Felix got up and put the cup in a drawer.

"The book goes on the fire."

It is not easy to burn a book. He was banging it down on the kitchen fire when Mr. Tracy walked into the house. Carston retreated backwards through the kitchen, where Felix pushed him into a cupboard, and kindly got him out again, and up the backstairs to the attic and left him alone with the bees. There he meditated on what was going on below, whether the bees would attack him, and what it would be like if they brought the old man up there.

Below, Scylla thought: 'Keep things amiable: keep things casual: pay out what rope we have.' She constrained Picus's father to breakfast, because his son was unwell, and noticed how Clarence slipped away to warn him, now that the worst had come to the worst.

"It was nice of you to come," she said—"just as the place is at its loveliest." Ross despised her for that, and Felix admired, while her spirit was falling away into pockets of pain like dropped heart-beats, because in everything Picus was a lie. Excepting under Gault Cliff, and they would never go there again. Never again. That brought up bubble upon bubble of agony each time they rose, with attention to the unpleasant details of his father's visit. That sinister antique was saying:

"Call that old nurse of yours. I want to ask her a question." And she did not dare to be anything but unspeakably civil, while he said:

"Did you unpack for Mr. Tracy, and if so did you find a green bowl in his case, or a book that wasn't a novel?"

Trust Nanna. She almost put Mr. Picus's father in his place. Felix's business to have done that. Felix had gone out. Oh, God! to collect more fish?

Ross helped: "Picus is pretty unwell. Shall I take you up?"

And she managed to say, coolly: "I don't see why a book not a novel or even a cup should be out of order in anyone's luggage. I could have asked Nanna that myself."

That bothered the old man's exit. Ross went too, and she sat alone, wondering where Carston had got to. "He's up with the bees, honey," said her nurse. Tell the bees. Nanna did that when one of them died. Which of them was going to die first?

Picus had taken his father's cup.

Picus had stunted its origin.

Picus had had an idea, or why the book?

Picus had run into small mystifications.

Picus had made love to her.

Picus would not make love again, because they had been found out.

Picus led Clarence a hard life.

No one could go to Picus and say: "So much for your silly devilries. *Turn ye to me.*" And I even thought of marrying him because of his beauty. I did not catch the joy as it flew. Damn female instincts. Picus should not have pretended it was the cup of the Sanc-Grail. That will do in weaker minds and more violent imaginations than mine and Ross's.

Meanwhile, Carston had discovered a dormer in the attic roof, and saw her walking the lawns. He stuck his head out, powdered with the shells of dead bees, and called. She ran in and up to the attic door.

"Couldn't you," he whispered, "get him over to Tollerdown to look for himself? Get Clarence to take him. That will give us time."

"Good," she said, "I'll go down and try it." They both saw that the real need was to get rid of the old man. But as she opened Picus's door, she heard:

"Go over to Tollerdown to satisfy myself. Why? You've got it and you can keep it. Would you like to know its history? In India it was the poison-cup of a small rajah I knew. He was poisoned, all the same, drinking out of it. I saw him with a yard of froth bubble coming out of his mouth. Burnt up inside, I believe. I brought it away and gave it to a lady, who was frequently at Tambourne when you were at school. When she contracted tuberculosis she had a fancy for it as a spitting-cup. That is, so far as I know, any interest that attaches to the thing."

"Your mother drowned herself, didn't she, Picus?" said Ross, with that impersonal interest in the event which was sometimes too strong an antiseptic, never a poison.

"Yes," said Clarence.

"You see," said the old man to his son—"since that is your selection from my collection you may as well know

your choice. You know now, and that your efforts to identify it as a mass-cup will hardly succeed."

"Picus," said Felix, "it is up to you to tell us if you have
this thing."

"You fool," said the old man, "I saw him take it, when
he thought I was asleep before the fire."

"What does it matter if he did, when we have none of
us seen the thing?"

Picus raised his shoulders out of the sheets:

"Oh, cut that, Felix, when it's where you put it, downstairs in the bureau drawer." They noticed the father in
the son. Then Scylla's turn came—"From the bridegroom
to the bride. Hardly as propitious as one would like."

"That is superstitious," said Ross,—"Scylla's no bride
for any son of yours, and the cup's bitter history concerns
no one but the dead."

"Why did he pretend it was the cup of the Sanc-Grail?"
said the old man.

"How did you pretend he did?" said Ross.

"A snip of an American called Carston told me last
night at Starn. Another candidate for your rather second-
hand beauties, Scylla—"

"Felix, will you fetch him?" said Ross.

Upstairs, through the bee-roar, Carston heard the boy
say:

"So you did give us away last night at Starn!"

"I'm damned if I did. That's his bluff." He thought: 'I
knew I'd have to go down. I'm in this. How life arranges
itself without our tugging and kicking.' "Give me a run-
over what's been said."

"He wants us to have it," said Felix. "It was a rajah's
poison cup. Jade is supposed to shew poison. Of course, it
doesn't, and the man died. I shouldn't be surprised if old
Tracy hadn't a hand in it. He brought it back and gave it
to a female tart. That was a bad story, because Picus's
mother pined about it, till they found her in the stream
beneath old Tracy's house. Picus was a kid at the time, and

he adored her, and the old man had the woman to live with him at Tambourne till she died of t.b., and the cup was one of her belongings. Sort of thing which wouldn't work out so badly to-day with divorces and fresh air. The old man's loving it; spotted that Picus has given Scylla the cup."

"Then why on earth the stunt about the spear and the well?"

"I don't know— He's the old man's son. Come down."

Carston felt his position false again. Somehow he had given a clue to this hag-driven ancient: he was a little in alliance with him: he protested. Picus's father said:

"Quite enough, my dear boy, quite enough. You were obviously startled, and I had my theory of what startled you. I'm sure Scylla will forgive you in time, and I must be off now. I'll leave you your treasure, but I should like my book on the mass-cups back. You see now that it will be quite useless to try and identify it from that."

"Ask Felix," said Picus. No one knew whether to help him out or not. Carston thought of its boards smouldering on the kitchen fire, making it, as Nanna had pointed out, unfit for proper use.

Scyllla said, coolly: "I can't part with the other half of my wedding-present."

And this infuriated the old man. It was evident, even to their over-hurried perceptions, that he was more than insulting and exultant, he was in earnest. He began to frighten them. They could not decide whether to economise the truth or not. The old man seemed in need of exorcism. A bib. Altogether too gothic now.

Then Felix cried out: "I burnt the damned thing when Carston told me that you and Picus were playing us up."

The old man began to laugh. "That'll do," he repeated. And quite soon after he was gone, and they dragged out chairs and lay on the lawn at different angles, no one wishing to speak.

Chapter XVII

CLARENCE FIGURED it out. Picus had done this to get away from him, falsifying the devotion of years, flaunt a pretty cousin, marry a pretty cousin: because she had some money: because she was a bird and bee woman: because Carston was after her, must be after her, or he would not have come back from Starn. Or why should any man run back after such an exit, to help a woman, a mime, a baggage, a bag of excrement? There is a great difference between a sportsman, a painter, a man that feels the earth, between Ross and Scylla and his terrible green Sdi creature, and Clarence's feeling for decoration best served by cities, a blasted heath no more than a site for his palace. He was on Carston and Felix's side, never satisfied with the earth sacrifice the others munched, wanting *décor* as Carston a stage. Picus was his set-piece, his jewel. His jewel had lied, his palace was unsound, the beautiful basket in which he had put all his eggs was broken. He had no more eggs to lay. A very serious man unable to exercise his sobriety, because he had made *fausse route* with his friend, because his education was insufficient for his abilities. Not for the first time he did not try to correct himself, thought about his wounds and his wishes until they took phantom shape and he slipped off uneasily with his gun down the wood. Scylla made a face after him. Ross shook his head. Carston had an impulse to follow.

"Gone off to invent excuses for Picus," said Felix, "for you to listen to— It's the occupation down here."

"Come and pose," said Ross. "I want a model."

Carston was alone with Scylla. He said:

"I think I've an excuse now to say 'explain a bit'." It was parching hot, gritty as if a storm of microscopic dust had filled up the holes in the leaves, in the grass-blades, in the skin.

"Reassure me, at least," he said, "that this would have happened without me."

"Of course. Much worse if it hadn't been for you." They stopped talking.

"I tried to help you," he said, "it is your turn." Saw the effort she made, thought how easy these people were to spur.

"Let's go up and tackle Picus," she said—"there is one thing about staying in bed, it runs to earth."

"No," said Carston, "you must excuse me. I've had about enough of that chap."

"So," said Scylla, "for the moment, have I."

"Seems to me he played a mean trick on you all— What I don't see is why. Or why it should have got you."

The other side of the house Ross was seeing Felix flung in a chair, hearing the nervous sobbing his own cool voice could not control. Nor could he control in himself his aversion to speak or to help.

"What in hell do we come here for? I told Scylla to sell those shares and we'd have been at Biarritz."

"It would have been the same at Biarritz."

"You might be. I should be different there. You're looking for something. I'm not. And I hope when you get it you'll like it. Looking for the Sanc-Grail. It's always the same story. The Golden Fleece or the philosopher's stone, or perpetual motion, or Atlantis or the lost tribes or God. All ways of walking into the same trap. And Scylla gets into bed with old Tracy's son."

"That is not the point. What is it about a trap?"

The boy got up and looked a little madly and very insolently at Ross, the blue eyes cold between lids red with weeping. Ross was surprised to find himself edging away, like a man who is to be shot at.

"We're through with the baby-brother business."

Upstairs, Picus had finished shaving, his body worked

on as delicately and scrupulously as a cat. Whistling to himself while Felix was sobbing, whistling back his power as their idol, like a god summoning an element or in confidence like prayer. He set his tie for the last time, shook himself, laid himself down on the window seat, and drew a ring with a pearl on to his atrociously powerful hand.

And Clarence out on the high turf was not looking at the sea or the terrible crest of Gault suspended in the haze. Or at the small enamel floor he trod on, flower and leaf stars and bars and rings and crosses: or at a dozen rabbits hurrying: or at one hawk not hurrying, until he dropped faster than the eye and there would be one rabbit the less. He walked slowly, inside himself, petting his phantoms, especially a phantom of Picus, the body up at the house was behaving more and more unlike. He wondered also why Scylla had called him "mediaevalist," because she said he assumed a form from inside and made things fit it, instead of compelling what is to do his construction for him. Hadn't Picus invented a lying fancy to please her, to get off with her? Lying and lecherous his bird was, for a woman who had snapped him up for her body's sake and her vanity. This went on until he saw the names he called her take body and walk to meet him out of the wood. Vanity, lechery, falsehood, and malice lolled along together across the grass, out of the trees. And because she called him mediaevalist, he saw them in archaic dress.

Scylla said to Carston on the lawn:

"So, you see, what sounded romantic excitement about the Sanc-Grail cup was real. And unfortunate?"

Carston wondered, deplored and detested the european faculty for taking the skeleton out of the cupboard. Rattling it, airing it, lecturing on it. She was winding up a discourse without enquiry into his feelings. On what he supposed was the skeleton, the world skeleton. He heard:

"If the materialist's universe is true, not a working truth to make bridges with and things, we are a set of blind factors in a machine. And no passion has any validity and no imagination. They are just little tricks of the machine. It either is so, or it isn't. If you hold that it isn't, you corrupt your intellect by denying certain facts. If you stick to the facts as we have them, life is a horror and an insult. Nothing has any worth, but to tickle our sensations and oil the machine. There is no value in our passions and perceptions, or final differences between a life full of design and adventure and a life crawled out in a palace or a slum. The life of Plato or Buddha, apart from the kick of the illusion, was as futile as the lives of the daughters of Louis XV. Old talk, you say, and remember *In Memoriam*. But notice what is happening now people have become used to the idea. Any little boy in a Paris bar, who never heard of physics knows. Everyone gets the age's temper. With results on their conduct— 'Why be good any more' they say, and the youngest ones not that. And it's not intellectual beauty the culture-camp admire. It's themselves for having such fine subconsciousnesses. Such an elegant sublimation of their infant interests. Watch the world with the skeleton acclimatised! Even when I was new we tried the bad to see if it might not be good. But the new lot aren't interested. Don't give a button for the good any more.

"And there is no evading it by any 'service of humanity' game. Unless you're one of the people who get sensual kick out looking after things, why help humanity? Think of Wells's Utopias. Birth-control, and peace and drains. And nothing left to do but report on the fauna of a further star. Our visiting-list extended to super-birds, or intellectually developed spiders. *Nothing* but physical adventure. Especially as we've picked up one priceless truth off the road, that every action brings with it its toxin and its antitoxin. If, instead of becoming cynical or scared, we started enquiry again from that—"

Felix shouted melodiously:

"I'm post-War. I'm just through getting clear of you. I admit you can scare me, but in reality you bore me. I don't care any more. I may be a mass of inhibitions, but I'm out for myself—"

Through the grilling haze, Luxury, Malice, and Untruth strolled over the grass to Clarence. In Ross's heart there twisted ache and dislike. Carston gave in to spiritual upset, while his body lay in a garden chair. Scylla ended:

"So even the memory of a great magic turned out to be a bird's joke."

Picus thought how he would appear downstairs and bewilder them again. Had enough of Scylla. Wished now he hadn't given her that cup. Caught out he'd been by the old man, but that wasn't over yet. Get right out and come in by another door. Make Clarence, Scylla, and the lot of 'em quite happy always. Play round his way and their way for ever. *And I'll give you leave to play till doomsday.* Not mother. Too late to do that. Sort of the old man's prisoner. Just thinking of that made him feel ill and want Clarence. Felix reached his finale.

"You've confused me very successfully, and you can put up with what I've become."

Scylla saw that Carston had had enough, and felt stifled and alone. Clarence returned in agony up the doubling wood-path, not the straight. Ross withdrew into his picture, and Carston hung on tight to a thought: 'We've all got to get out of here for a bit.'

Chapter XVIII

"TIRED," SAID Scylla, changing her dress, and leaving that to stare out at the wood— "Tired of your wretched beauty, your rearrangements of light on a leaf."

"Bored," said Picus, who had gone to meet Clarence and missed him. And he meant sad. And Clarence, giving Nanna a hand skinning the rabbits he had shot, looked at his bloody hands: "I suppose I've got a broken heart and these wretched feelings come in through the holes."

"Alone," said Felix, "when I've got away it'll be the same."

Only Ross embraced his solitude, thought of the shape of each thing he drew, until the earth seemed one growing stillness, of innumerable separate tranquillities, for ever moving, for ever at rest.

Unfortunately the members of the house-party were not behaving like that. An organic view of Felix, for instance? He damned the scene—knew that he had handled it without imagination. Besides, the boy should be wearing his "youth's gay livery" before a livelier audience than hills and the sea.

And there was more coming through than Picus's wiles, life opening like the unfolding of a scene. An endless screen of coromandel lacquer, the design travelling with it, fold in, fold out. Enough for Ross to know that there was design and seize the detail, a man content with the tangible, piece by piece, to whom no single object was dumb. He thought of the brickness of a brick until he seemed aware of it throughout, not side after side or two or three, but each crumb of its body, and each crumb reduced to its molecular construction, until the brick ceased to be a cube and could as easily be reformed again.

And the only prayer to which he condescended was that Scylla would keep her head since there were hysterics about; then left the studio and joined the party now slowly regathering on the lawn. All but Felix. Carston did not know how to greet Picus, not it seemed in any disgrace, and telling them a story about a parson's wife.

"So she knitted me a check sweater, and I had a pain. And I lay flat on the grass, and told a curate and another curate to play chess on my back. And I found a caterpillar and made them make love."

"They don't," said Ross, "it's the butterflies."

"These did. And the first curate said check with the white bishop, and I stopped enjoying it, and hunched up and went in to get my tea, and there was a party, and I stopped thinking."

"When do you do your thinking?"

"Never."

Scylla said: "I wish you had, before you let this morning's business be sprung on us. What did you do it for?"

They all waited for his answer. It came.

"Mind your own business." Like a rude boy. And then:

"It was my mother who was driven to death."

"That's nothing to do with it," said Ross.—"Pawn your father's collection. Throw it into the sea, but don't—"

"Don't what?" said Picus.

Felix came out.

"Here's what's left of your bloody book. Nanna took it off the fire." Ross opened it with kind hands not afraid of char-black and turned the middle pages the fire had not curled up. He stared.

"Look at this." The book was open at a full-page photograph of the cup. Underneath was written—*Plate* 17. *Early English altar-vessel. From the collection of Christopher Tracy, Esq.*

While the cup was fetched from its drawer and passed from hand to hand, Carston appreciated Picus's blissful look, untouched by relieved anxiety, not too elated or even too absorbed.

"Picus," said Ross, "in common decency tell us what you know.

"Now that I've been asked, listen. I took the cup. Mother and I used to pretend with it. Not this time, but when I came back to Tollerdown last spring. The well was brimming and I took it out to get a drink, and it slipped through my fingers like a fish. It couldn't be got out then, and I didn't want Clarence to fuss. He didn't know. Once it was gone, I wondered what it was, and I this time told my father that I hadn't seen it lately, and something he said put me on to that book. So I left it to see what would happen. And Felix fished it out with Clarence's spear. It may have come from India. The whore who killed my mother may have used it. It suited the old man to palm it off as a church vessel and to tell you it was a poison-cup. He's lived in India long enough, and his best friend is an arch-deacon. That's all I know. Oh yes, I curled up behind an ant-hill on Hangar's ridge Carston shied at. And I stuck the cup in his room to teach him that ants don't bite, and give him something else to think about. Oh yes, I made love to Scylla because she is a darling, and usually I'm afraid of women. And—"

"Hold up—" said Ross.

It was a great blessing that the old man had done the lying. Put untruth away in a far corner. Far corners are more difficult to get at. But what they needed then was Picus's brightness restored.

Carston said: "It seems to me that your father's story was a lie because he wanted the book back."

"Trust Nanna," said Scylla, blissfully, "she wouldn't have the kitchen fire put out."

"The kitchen fire, mark you," said Felix, suddenly interested again.

Hestia is an old goddess—I think she had a name written under her altar not even the Romans might know. And in her case, their lives, the sap of their bodies was nourished at Nanna's fire. There the sea bubbled in butter, the meat dripped its red juice, birds split into white shreds. Round it the lettuces sparkled, the roots under the wood boiled, old herbs scented the place, wine dripped in like dew, and Nanna was perhaps the only person unequivocally loved.

The wailing that went up round her: "Nanna, I'm hungry." "Nanna, I've got a cold." "Nanna, I've blistered my heel." "Nanna, where are the buttons on my white waistcoat?" Nanna who liked cigarettes and silk stockings and no device for saving labour, her hair tied up like an old gipsy, and her tongue free. She had got them round this corner. All the same, a lie is harder to run to earth three counties away.

"We are left where we began," said Felix, "with the Thoroughly Rum."

Also, as Carston noticed, with the thoroughly boring. The adventure of the cup had happened. It had been complicated, violent, inconclusive. Now it would be too much trouble to take trouble for more trouble. For a new series of untruths or "stubborn, irreductible" facts. Not much chance of them, and difficult to get. Three counties away. As though they had been in a room together, and something had passed through that had left too raw traces for all its invisibility, had left them alone with private griefs and memories quickened. Which, if it came again, would enter by a different door. Picus, stirred by the story of his mother, victim of victorian social stupidities in an age less agreeable and more remote than that which produced mass-cups, and complicated biographies of public characters like Huon of Bordeaux, son of Julius Caeser, and Morgan le Fay.

They were tired of it, as he saw, till another door opened. This, when his own interest for the first time was really aroused. The business was more or less out in the open. News. A story. He wanted to find out exactly what Mr. Tracy had been up to. If they were prepared to leave it alone until something else happened, he was not; anticipating a dateless, glorious moment when he would appear before them with the story complete. Hand them the finished psychology of old Mr. Tracy. A new philosophy: a fortune: the cup of the Sanc-Grail. No intention of leaving now.

Then a sound that was almost "service" rose in his thought. Not public or personal or progressive, or in relation to the "hard-eyed men of the Y.M.C.A." Not even for results; there might be no results. As the conception grew, fortifying like a cup of wine *à point*, he saw an approach to Scylla, without reference to possession or to her reaction. What she did not have with these unemployed condottieri her peers. What he must do for her, and she was no spoilt american bitch.

Immediately, he stepped into another world, their world and his own. At its largest, airiest and freest. He had never been there before. He had always been there. He would always be there, never the same apprehensive, gifted, rootless man. Reckoning without his hosts, he urged another slice of cake on her, and suggested that it might be his turn to fetch the evening fish.

"We'll go together," she said. "A walk will do me good."

Chapter XIX

I T WAS PERCEPTIBLY cooler, stale-cool, uneasy air-threads stirring in the straight wood drive. No sun since three o'clock, but a glaring grey gauze overhead. Outside the wood, below the little cliff, a small scoop of bay protected the fisherman's boats. From the edge they could have stepped on to the roof of his hut, whose tarred shingles were frosted with salt. Set on a ledge out of storms' reach, brambles padded it from the cliff's side, and it was reached down wooden balks, steep-set and built into the clay. It surprised Carston to see the egg-blue and peacock water changed to the colour of a gun-barrel. Little wind, but the sea was twitching, slapping against the rocks; the colours inland, neither light-veiled or shining, but off a new palette.

Scylla was staring out to sea, and her head lifted in profile made her look at the sky, where it seemed as if some mathematical monster had risen out of the west. For where the sun was turning down-Channel, a ball glared, surrounded by ranks of rose bars, and out from these clouds radiated that reached over to the eastern heavens, across whose spokes strayed loose flakes dipped in every variety of flame, the triangles of empty sky stained all the greens between primrose and jade.

"Herring sky," she said.

"What does that mean?"

She laughed with a confident joy he understood the first time.

"South-west wind. Listen!" He heard his heart beating, a hair in his ear, and a trans-finite length away, the stirring that had made uneasy the sea.

"A big storm," she said, turning on him eyes full of an

animal's pleasure. Round the point where the day before he arrived they had played at Aphrodites, a boat came dipping back, the bowsprit dancing and dripping, where over the deep-travelling reef the sea had begun to coil under and over.

"Harris is back in time. We're in for it. No more fish." A note in her brain about the fish problem. More too freshly killed meat. Picus and Felix on the subject. Then the only good poem a bad poet ever wrote, anticipating jazz:

> *"When descends on the Atlantic*
> *The gigantic*
> *Storm-wind of the equinox."*

He took her hands and they rocked, saying with her:

> *"From Bermuda's reefs and edges*
> *Of sunken ledges*
> *On some far-off bright Azore*
> *From Bahama and the dashing*
> *Silver-flashing*
> *Surges of San Salvador."*

Fallen into nature with her. For the first time in his life. Good old Gulf Stream.

Harris the fisherman had downed his main-sheet, flung out an anchor and was rushing a dinghy to shore.

"Take your fish, Madame Taverner, it's the last you'll see. I've got my pots to get in."

"We'll help."

Two minutes later Carston was in a dinghy in a slightly resentful scoop of sea, and spent an ungrateful hour hauling up lobster-cages filled with kicking, pinching sea cardinals, ink blue; and the humanitarian protest came from Scylla when they were tossed into a cauldron bubbling on the stones, in an angle of the little secret cliff where England rose out of the harvested sea.

The wood was darkish, fearful and sad, until they saw

the windows shut and already lit, a fire leaping up made out of the driftwood he had helped haul up. Blue sparks and white and green, wind shifting about outside in the trees, until with a scream the up-Channel gale was loosed and they became creatures couched under a stone that quivered in the uproar and mounted to bed with candles streaming.

Carston lay in bed and heard above the thunder a gull repeating itself. "Ai, ai," it said, up somewhere in the tumbling sky, a little noise laid delicately upon the universal roar of air. The house was strong, he thought, its stone thrilling but not a window that rattled, tapped by their climbing roses.

There were pockets in the wind when he could hear the sea. A crash, then under-roar and scream of pebbles, the ravelled water dragged. A light-patch fell on his floor, a piece of the late moon racing apparently from a cloud whipped off her, and behind her a star or so, unhurried, observant and indifferent on a night when everything was out and about. He looked out to sea, surprised that it appeared no more than a bright silver lacquer, when water mountains should have been moving in.

Scylla alone wondered how the wood below Gault was bearing it, flooded with salt water, heaped with seaweed, the little stream choked with wrack.

Dark again in Carston's room. A rain-flaw drummed on the panes. Then with a shriek the wind sprang again. He could not hear the gull, but a few seconds later a crack and a long crash, knew it was a tree gone, and looking out in the next moon-interval, saw something altered in the outline of the wood. It disturbed him to think how hopeless the dawn would be, the 'dew silky' quiet changed for grey air, spray-salted on the lips. Would the others enjoy it? Would it blow the nonsense out of them? They might be house-bound for days. Oh, God! He was wondering how to prevent this when he fell asleep.

Chapter XX

Breakfast reassured him how far they minded the
weather. They had been out and there was news, a
tramp aground on Tunbarrow Ledges, and twenty-three
drowned men laid out on tables in the parish room.

"A danish boat," said Scylla. "Does anyone here speak
it?"

Carston did, but did not see that it was his duty to say
so in order to assist what was left of the crew, who must
have a consul somewhere. He bore it when Scylla took him
out down the wood, quiet under a colonnade, until they
came out and staggered against a wall of air.

The little bay disappointed him, packed with dull drift
that choked the waves, a pocket for the storm's mess, and
on the headland they found the sea racing, but not with
the explosion he had imagined up the cliff's side.

"Tide's out." So that formless bright patch of moon
was still pulling the sea about, holding it off the land. Then
she led him carefully to the edge, and he saw a hole in the
clay, blue, raw and dripping from a wave's mouth.

"That came out last night."

Still the sky travelled, torn cloud and blue enough for
trousers, rain-flaws, and air ribbons. The wildness ener-
vated him. The excitement was cerebral, all spectacle, a
whip-up for the eyes and the salt-refreshed palate, the
ears cut off from common sounds.

At lunch words crossed his wind-filled head like the
gull's cry in the night. The well at the cottage on Tollerdown would be filling; floating corpses could be skimmed
off: the vicar at Tunbarrow was reliable with the ship-
wrecked: Felix had gone over there.

While they relaxed over coffee, the boy came in, bareheaded, strapped into oilskins, pale, his cheeks burning with two red circles exercise would not account for.

"Eaten?" said his sister.

"I don't want to. I've seen them."

"Seen what?"

"Twenty-three dead men." They all reacted to the young voice horror and drama made unsteady.

"Singularly drowned with their wounds shewing—where the fish gnawed—"

"Haven't had time to be gnawed," said Ross. "Don't overdo it."

"I saw them till they had no significance whatever, because I saw death. I suppose you admit they're dead?"

"A death," said Ross, coldly, "you court yourself in the cutter year in, year out. We court. What about it?"

Felix swallowed, and stared right and left.

"Death's family party," he said. "I've seen it. Getting nearer home. Don't you know you're in league with that sort of thing? And that your shifts for getting away are hopeless—"

"What shifts?" said his sister. "Ease up, boy, stop running round in circles. I didn't drown them."

He addressed himself to her:

"Your love affairs—what are they worth? and your famous strength that supports us? I know you're a strong woman, with your stunt of opening doors every sane person knows are better shut. I'm your brother and you'll not take me in. Twenty-three bodies, twenty-three pictures of death have taught me the worth of your tricks. And I don't flatter myself I shall do anything on my own. You've sucked me too dry for that—"

Carston saw her swing the crystal slung from her neck he knew the boy had given her.

"Dearie," said Picus, "let your back hair down, and be yourself."

"Go away," said Ross.

"Go and look for what you want where you think you'll

find it," she said. Temperately, ineffectually, the reserve shewing how she loved him.

Carston wanted to kick him. Clarence yawned. The boy took no notice. Carston thought: 'Ways of clearing the house. A full well at Tollerdown, and Biarritz the brighter by one cub.' Whose adieux were being made separately.

"And Clarence can nurse his fancy heart-break and Picus his second-rate chic. And Ross make his appetites serve his art, or whichever way round he does it. And Carston get kick out of being taken in by our fake aristocracy. And Nanna slave and tell you how wonderful you are. I'm going where there won't be any more fairy-stories, and my complexes can rot me or—"

"All right," said his sister, "we'll try not to overwork Nanna, or impose on Carston too much."

'Well, well,' thought the latter: 'the new type of child: Biarritz, bars. *What every little boy in a bar knows.* And how far had her love got Scylla?' His new-found confidence working easily in him, he smiled at Felix.

"'Portrait of the artist as young man,'" he said. "Good luck."

But the boy answered:

"D'you fancy my sister so much that you've learned her tricks? She is keeping them for someone else than me, that's all."

She wondered as she left the room, and for once ordered Nanna to iron his linen immediately, if his version of the truth was refreshing him, as any contact should. And, pitifully, how long it would last. And anxiously, what he would do. And, maliciously until she felt better what sort of a fool he would make of himself, what gaping mouth would snap him up.

So he lost her until he should come to look for her, Grail vanished, girl and all.

Incidentally, he settled which of the rest should go or stay. Next day, contrary to custom, the wind fell, and a torrent of soft mist packed in rain brimmed the land, refilled ceaselessly off the falling sea as it passed in over the hills. They could hear the water slowly thundering and not much else but their rather distressed voices. Carston alone had the serenity of plans. After he had persuaded Scylla to go up to London, Clarence said that he would go over to the cottage or the dust and damp would get in and annoy his young man. Picus had gone already, flitted off, the raining fog hiding him for a time. Carston meant the same landscape to swallow him on the trail of old Mr. Tracy. He asked Ross for his plans.

"Stay here and get on with things. I'll wait till you come back."

FELIX

Felix bolted black and stormy to his hotel and emerged again into the gold light, fresh as roses. He crossed the river, and on the brink of the Champs-Élysées felt the rhythm of Paris begin to stir him and caress. A movement of tireless youth, each instant crystallized a century, illustrated by details small and intimate, grandiose or chic. His lost goodness returned, recomposed out of adoring attention, until like a polished bay, the Place de la Concorde opened before him. There the fragile Paris façades grouped themselves round the bronze ladies washing their faces, round a boy wandering out among the skimming taxis, in love.

He walked some way before he remembered that he had a rendezvous with a person as well as Paris, and turned back along the Rue de Rivoli, drowned in the evening sky. He had forgotten what he had left behind, novice at his first ceremony of mystery, he turned up the Rue Boissy d'Anglas and found himself indoors again.

His friend was with a band. Felix hated bands. No setting for him when he felt that he was not really there. He knew he had an inferiority complex, but there were too many draped legs and wrapped coats, and he might not have heard the last story, would have to pretend it had arrived stale from London. He would be found out, and no one would care how he loved Paris, or how much he knew about art. And with what was left of his generous simplicity, he did not count at all on his clothes which were the original of many replicas, or on his money, which was not borrowed.

Here was a different kind of loneliness. With his own generation, not as at home with the half-generation ahead. Loneliness all the same, self-imposed. In the french-american group he was a distinguishable figure. Boys fresh as roses in a shop-window, as picked and perfect. Only a close observer might have said that Felix was still on his bush. Or having left it, that his stalk was not down in the water.

How to pretend to be the devil you are afraid to be.

How to be a grand seigneur on nothing a year.

How to be yourself when you do not know that self, and are afraid to find out.

How to get tight when you don't do it regularly.

The café walls were black, filled with mirror panels squared with small red and gold lights. Like an old mirror that has a circle of miniature mirrors inlaid in its glass, the place reflected and repeated a great deal of what is going on in the world. And Felix, with his letter of introduction, could not pull it out, with his pass behind the scene over his heart, could not present it. He forgot the walk he had taken, fell back into the easy trick of disapproval, mask for longing to be a little king in that bright crowd. King over a french boy, pencilled like a persian miniature, discreet and gentle as a cat. Shut absolutely in his race, yet escaping it by an indescribable sweetness, a perfume of goodness uncorrupted by intelligence which would last—how long? Felix told himself that his complexion could not last long anyhow, and retired on a loud excuse to dust a little powder on his own fair nose and chin. Never be able to impress that boy, who was neither in authority or out, who wore his youth for a fairy-cloak which for Felix was a naked skin.

Nor the buddha-shaped musician from the Midi, loved for his wit, serving his turn with each of them in turn as though they were not there. Felix turned to the boy he had come to see, the adorable American who knew everybody. He wondered if he was after all another Carston. (Felix had underrated Carston, having no experience between the man from Boston and his friend from the Middle

West.) He was smarter than any Carston, brimmed up with sap and impudence, a boy who, if he had come from the moon, would have made his friends dream until he taught them not to. On whom, if Felix had known it, Scylla reckoned for vengeance. He was glad enough to see Felix, wear him for a night or so in his cap. Remember him as a spoiled, sweet girl remembers. Felix would have the money for several parties and was an authentic specimen. He would give him his turn.

They all spoke French better than he, who always wanted to do it too well, whose ear was not in tune. His next brandy went down, and as his brain quickened he heard a party being discussed for late that night. Would they ask him? How could he bear it if they didn't? In reality it did not occur to the Frenchmen that he would not want to go to Montmartre, and did not know how to take care of himself. Not that they were interested—the brandy mounted darkly—nobody was interested. Their pure speech hummed like a dynamo. He stretched himself insolently and spoke to a bulb-cheeked yellow-haired child there pursuing the career, and impressed by Felix's obvious need to do nothing of the sort.

The party began to discuss a well-known eccentric who had just left.

"Oh, that man—" said Felix, gladly. But his comments in pretentious French were too severe, and left the others in doubt whether he really knew him. Soon they were not listening, and he saw the Frenchwoman catch his friends's eye. Only the bulb-cheeked child was still attentive. Little *faux monnayeur*, fresh from his lycée, still rather ingenuous, he helped Felix along his transitions of envy, wonder, and fear.

A russian boy came in, tight in a merry circle of private intoxication, small, black, asiatic head in air. He sang:

> "*Si par hazard tu vois ma tante,*
> *Compliments de ma part.*"

A baby-faced negro rolled his drum. The saxophone began to cough out variations, apparently played backwards, on *Dinah Lee*. His memory of the sweet tune pricked a bubble in the boy's petulance. He asked the Frenchwoman to dance, and moving easily with her, a little drunk, he began to bubble praise of Paris. When they got back, the little bar off the dancing-room was roaring with the love of life. In a frieze along the bar, in squares and fives and sixes round the scarlet tables were all the right people to play with. People of the world and the half-world, people who found the arts useful, and a fair number of people who were found useful by the arts. Eminent eccentrics, the very poor, the very rich, capital in wits or youth or looks or wit; diversity of creatures, young society in action, the motif of the time and the place repeated in the exit and entry of the pick of Paris' basketful of boys. It was Felix's party, too, if he could have forgotten himself, let himself go, torn up his silly little mask. Instead, he allowed himself to feel home-sick, looked timidly at his friend who had caught the eye of a princess, and was making her sure she was pleased to have caught his.

"Let's have a day in the country to-morrow. We might go to Versailles."

"All right, if we're up." The voice was soft and virile, touched with a brogue. No getting him to himself where everyone was out to be seen. In desperate need of a focus he gave up trying to understand French, and began to describe the people at his table to himself. He would never get to know them. Who ever gets to know the French? He might as well have something to remember. When he was a famous man, they'd wish they'd been nicer to him. There was the Frenchwoman in her man's coat, without make-up, half-boy, half great lady, level-eyed and low-voiced, incapable of pretention or any false gesture. Then the musician's chinese rotundity, the pouting lips, flat and amiable white hands, contradicted by a chin cleft like a Caesar's, and terribly intelligent eyes. Felix respected those eyes.

They had looked at him kindly, and he suspected pity, found himself caught with an emotion that was like pity when he looked at the third, the young Frenchman, because his beauty was "no stronger than a flower." Scented like one, too, out of a bottle Felix wanted the name of. —"But he's no brains," he said, "and they say he takes drugs. It's a pity." He nursed the idea that he could be happy nowhere. Was there any one else in the room who was alone? He looked around. Even two boys having a row at the bar were in contact. A swing door burst open. It was the Russian back again, if anything, tighter. Felix saw a glass of champagne beginning to slide on the top of the downy black head. Skull of a tibetan idol: mouth of a wicked baby. In the middle of the floor he lowered the glass, and began an on-the-spot Charleston. "Hey, hey," he shouted. Then a rune:

> "O qu'il est beau, mon village,
> Mon Paris,
> Mon Paris."

He shot through to the dancing-room. He was ugly. He had exquisite hands and feet. 'Probably a shop-assistant pretending to be a prince.' Felix's demon was on the spot. He came back again, carrying the glass now like a chalice, empty, and looking crossly into it. Felix burst out laughing.

"Excuse me," he said, "have another drink," and went with him to the bar.

"Enfin il s'amuse, le petit anglais," said the musician. Felix's friend frowned. Money spent on that demon would not last long. But Felix had sensed that here was another isolation, but not its quality, its brutal and innocent acceptance of things. But he was talkable-to, with his unmodulated French, his trick of sprawling sideways at the bar, his head pitched forward, laughing down at his feet.

ROSS

Ross finished the drawing of a plant that grew in whorls and spirals and tendrils and bracts. The naturalist had trained the painter. He copied it exactly. To-morrow he would do it differently, double it, halve it, add six to it, make a picture out of repetitions of a stalk.

It was very late. The hardly perceptible noise of his pencil was all he had for company. He went into the kitchen to look for bread and cheese. A candle was lit in a tin lantern, there was a fire-stain on the floor. Nanna, long in bed, had left her sewing.

> *There was an old woman and she sat spinning,*
> *And still she sat and still she span, and still she wished for*
>   *company.*

He grinned at the old nurse's horror-story, went back to the studio and watered one of the shallow pans stuck with the seeds he had gathered tramping Europe. A bee-orchid had come up: an odd-scented herb from a pass on the Pyrenees: a rare lily was over. Whenever he touched it life grew. Plants and dogs and children. Eggs hatched. And men? They were there to make him laugh. If they found rest in him, he was indifferent as Nature, and in general as kind.

He loosened the earth pricked by a hairy spike, tossed a pebble away, opened a window. A bird disturbed brushed him without alarm. An owl sailed by, curved over at the house-corner and skimmed down the wood. A dark grey night, brimming with business. His portfolio under his arm for a picture-book, he went up to bed.

PICUS

On the same night Picus went out, also alone and in a clearing among trees. English yews, black and untidy with their shoots that are never young, a yard of rusty twig, old as a house-high lime or beech.

The space was diversified with the stone boxes of a country churchyard. Dressed for Piccadilly, Picus was lying face-down on his mother's grave, on turf not dew-sown, but rain-sodden, overlooked by a sugar-white marble angel carrying an urn. He was telling the stalks and the worms and a snail how he loved her, and resented her death, and was troubled by its mystery.

'Pretty mother, why did you do it?'

'Why did that tart matter?'

'What did you want me to do?'

'Why do I hate all women?'

Once Nanna had made him ill when he had heard her say: "What did Mrs. Tracy mean by drowning herself with Mr. Picus a boy, and his father taking his child to the inquest and saying it was suicide?"

And Scylla's answer: "People went in for sensibilities then." Blaming his mother. Now he'd see if she had any. He grasped the turf mound and tried to shake it. Get mother out and make her tell him what had really happened and that he must never make anyone suffer as she had suffered. That was like his father and he must never be like his father— The marble parody of a nymph went on offering him an urn. He tried to see if the lid would come off, but it was all in one meanly designed, badly chiselled piece. His father with his impeccable taste had stuck it up on purpose. Fattened on his son's hatred. Had used the cup to make him wicked. To lose him the people who comforted him. Would go on living forever. The wires of the rust tin flower-box caught his cuff. Rain water in it, and no flowers. Can't go daisy-hunting at midnight in the rain. That's all mother had, an empty tin box with the rain in it and no flowers. He did not count his six feet of young man flung there.

"You'd no business to go off and leave me like that. Gives me nothing to do but want you back. Just for a minute to tell me something: put kick into me again. Mummy, don't you see: you gave the old boy the game? You were so much prettier: might have stayed and seen me through. Now you've made me be a bitch."

He sat there weeping and considering how he had been a bitch and couldn't stop. Didn't know how to find old Clarence and Scylla again and love them and see that they loved him. Clarence now. One of his suspicions was that the change in Clarence was his fault. Why wasn't it entirely the man's own fault if he chose to go gaga and mope about like a frustrated hen? Funny. They used to call Clarence a bit too handsome, like a super-chorus-boy. Now you might say like a butler with a past. Tell him that. Now Felix beginning to act like a toad. Good old Carston. And great Ross. Hats off to Ross, doing nothing at all but what he had to. He remembered their old conviction that Ross had some sort of stable tip in invisible affairs. 'Won't tell. Says we can look at his pictures.'

'We should have been all right together, Scylla and I, and now the sight of her scares me stiff. Lovely and witty, and decent and passionate and kind. There's a figure that stands sentinel before her. I can't see its face. Not a chap you'd care to meet. If I looked at him, he'd go.'

'These things matter a devil of a lot, and they don't matter at all.'

'Scylla's a darling. Want my Scylla.'

'Mother, why can't I have Scylla?'

The angel went on holding the urn. He kicked the turf till a sod tore off. A glow-worm turned its back on him. By infinite degrees the green gem moved off.

'And for half a minute I thought that cup had come to light us up a bit.' He whistled *Waiting for the moon to rise*.

'And it was the old man after all!'

'And Carston shan't have Scylla if he does call the old man's bluff.'

He had the usual difficulty in extracting the glow-worm from the grass.

'Go and light up mummy's tomb.' He stuck it round the knob of the urn, where it fell off. He kicked the muffled earth that squelched, the tears pouring down, till he found a cache of pebbles under his heel and pelted the marble female in the thick dark, and then he had another idea, and with a handful in his pocket went across, round and over the graves, to a low, unlighted house, and tossed them up against a window. A head poked out:

"What's that?"

"Me."

"Come in, my dear boy, come in." An old man in a nightshirt opened his front-door and let him in.

WHEN WE WERE VERY YOUNG

While Felix was whirling down from Montmartre in a taxi with the boy friend and the Russian, all of them drunk. Different drunks. The boy friend roaring gay, the world forgiven because of midsummer Paris, crossed with his original irish love of a spree. He beamed, an arm round Felix, an arm round the Russian whom he usually detested.

"I've got a new crab."

"Let's go and christen it."

"What shall we call it?"

"Aloysius."

"Où allons-nous pour le baptême?" Felix suddenly pitched sideways, his forehead on the Russian's knees.

"I speak it a bit, Boris," he said. It was true. The American felt too jolly to be angry even at the unknown tongue. And Felix knew that he had found what he had come for, this slip out of Russia, a burning black pillar of congenial romance. Birth and ruin and exile, and a name not like green hills, but a wild, snow-crested tree. He would take Boris away. He would go back with Boris into Russia. He would take Boris home. He had found what he had come to find. Not the other one, who, after all, wasn't a gentleman. An awful, delicious fear that Boris could read his mind, had heard his last thought and was amused by its stupidity. While the American sobered up to be surprised at Felix, all his high and mighty airs melted before that notorious lost wolf-cub. God only knew what sort of a not bad sort originally, but finished by having to live on its wits. And Boris was a trifle embarrassed, observant, indifferent, and thoroughly enjoying himself. An evening after his own heart.

They were on the shore of the Place de la Concorde, this time an empty sea. The taxi raced across its grey glass, over the arc of a bridge, and began to thread old Paris like a furious shuttle.

"*O bel! O gai!*" whispered Felix, upright now between them, his dark blue eyes turned stars. Both admired him a little, nervously. Both profoundly hoped he'd enough money on him, the Russian because he had none, the American because he had no intention of spending any he had. And Felix saw Europe folk-wandering, and how out of the movements of the peoples he had found his companion, young and wicked, and in need and kind. Like a bow bent and relaxed, and strung with fresh arrows, his desires took purpose. At a ghastly little mixed bordel, he walked in like a prince come home.

SCYLLA

She arrived in London at the time when all reasonable
citizens are trying to leave it, and the place seems fuller
than ever. Full of townspeople shewn up by the
magnificence of summer, with children who appear bru-
talised from want of contact with things growing; where,
in spite of every grit-weathered leaf, there is a pretence
made that all is for the best inside the vast, roaring, fortui-
tous wilderness: that Epping Forest is the true green wood,
and Southend virgin sea. If Paris is a lovely salon displayed
for conversation, London is a lumber-room to be foraged
for junk, rubbish, white elephants, treasure. Midsummer
is not the time to do it.

Scylla walked through the green park, fresh from no
substitute hills and the sea, and not in the least grateful for
them. Yet with only contempt for the posters and pretence
that represented the Londoners' poor escape to the land.
Her yellow lawn frock blew up over her knees, under her
powdered arms and throat there was a faint gold patina
of freckles. Her little neck-scarf flying out behind her, she
walked like a nymph in a temper, blessing nothing she
passed.

Something had been taken away from her. Not Picus
or Felix, but what they had made her think about. Apples
of Iduna the goddess, given her to feed the Aesir, without
which she pined without dying. What happened to Iduna
and her apples after? Loki, Saturday, had stolen them and
shut her up in a giant's castle, and she had been waited
on by elf-women, very pleasant in front, but round the
back made out of hollow boards. Beastly hot day and no
adventures. Business at grey offices in Lincoln's Inn. The
only woman she really liked married to a boy she did not.
She was going to dinner there.

She remembered that the woman, her friend Lydia,

had wanted once to marry Clarence. Might have married him until, one day, Clarence had made a scene: said that he could not leave Picus: that Picus needed him: had told Lydia that she did not love him: that it was a trick to get a husband: and had broken down badly after. Lydia had said nothing. And 'had never been quite the same since.' That said it exactly. Had probably married her slick young outsider to annoy Clarence. A real chorus-boy beauty with a spirit to match. She would dine there, in their pretentious flat, all shams. It pleased Lydia if her friends flattered her husband. Scylla knew that it might please her that evening if she shewed contempt.

So no sweet temper adorned her as she swung into the new sitting-room with its faked cabinets and painful majolicas, and saw Lydia in a too-short frock and a too-tight hair wave, and a too-pink make-up, reading the *Romaunt de la Rose*. A woman bred out of great stone castles for a life of power and danger, she looked a fool, stripped of what should have been on her, the formal setting that should have extended north, south, east, and west of her. Not necessarily castles. A bare table and a window stuffed with sacking might have suited her purpose, when the purpose was her own, not a stunt to please her husband, like a lion riding a bicycle at a fair.

Vexed deliberation marked the ivory forehead, her chief beauty. Her stockings were not drawn tight, and did not match. An intelligence made for children and learning and administration was adapting itself to marriage, with a gigolo, in a shaky business, in London, without capital, after the war. Would do it badly unless she broke him. Could not break him, he would twist and slip off.

A cathedral had better not turn mouse-trap, or a chalice a cocktail shaker. A ten-inch gun should not be trained on a mark that is not there.

And Scylla found that all she could do was laugh to see her friend so much in love.

And Lydia knew this. Also that Scylla had kept her freedom, was up to all their old amusements out in Europe, down in the South. Scylla saw Clarence continually and made fun of him. Might flirt with him, more curious things can happen, when her proper business was to marry too, and establish herself.

And both the young women knew that this meeting if inevitable was unfortunate, the end of a friendship from university to marriage. Lydia had made a dangerous one. God only knew where adventure would lead the other.

The husband came in. Knocked over his wife's book with a movie paper, and began to talk about himself. A row at the garage and how he had scored. Lydia frowned.

"Phil, Scylla is here." He kissed Scylla several times, while she stared up to see what the prettier woman could do with her eyes; while she was loathing him because he had taken her friend away from her. To use Lydia's practical brain and her unpractised love for his own little ends, to betray her, mishandle her, exploit her. And be dreadfully punished when Lydia recovered from her passion because he had laid familiar paws on her pride. Her heaven-born pride which might as easily move to hell. In a timeless instant she saw the woman Lydia would be, when she would punish her fancy-boy for being the slick little animal he was. And, during the transition, break both hearts.

I may become like that, too. A thought passing, passionate then dispassionate.

At lunch, on Philip's insistence, she praised the table-setting, who had adored Lydia for being the world's worst housekeeper. It was easier when Philip dropped the garage and making eyes, and shewed frank jealousy. He was really afraid of his wife's old friends, knew that he must detach her from them quickly. And Lydia revelled in his authority, her mind storing it up for later, for part of the interminable, intolerable score they would have to recite to one another.... In a house where there would be no children, nor any garden for forgiveness full of the other's favourite flowers.

Now Scylla minded this. Minded also that Philip had not even thought to approach her as his wife's friend. What was left her now but observation? She had had enough of grief. There was only her amusement left, the contrast between Lydia's naïve eroticism and her formidable wits: Philip's technique with her no more than the length of rope on which he had to hang himself. His method was to cut conversation, to interrupt whatever was said; and when he spoke, interrupt himself, so that there should never be any continuity. Perfectly sound. The quickest way to exasperate Scylla. He was reckoning that he could, not quite such a fool as these grand ladies thought him. Could shew them that not being a gentleman was worth something: give Lydia's lady friend something else to call him than a misplaced insect.

And Scylla no longer believed that her reserve of charity was an arsenal. She did not want Lydia if she could not tell her the story of the cup, draw on her learning, and on her instinct for tradition, which might have been created to meet the situation. Without that story her summer in the South was no story, and how often had Lydia been down with them in the wood? Philip once, had followed her there, uninvited, and found her singing them troubador songs. Had bawled jazz and almost dragged her away. Impulses cold, cruel, and insolent grew in Scylla, along with understanding perfecting itself.

A new aspect of the worst had arrived. They were already too accustomed to it. Had seen too many designs broken, whose assembly had been mysteries of harmony. Until they had forgotten unity, harvest ahead of vintage; forgotten that there could be any condition but emulation, advantage, and personal success. She despised herself because she had not the clean surgery to cut out memory and hope. As the story of the house could not be told without the wood, the house-party could not be described without the cup. As well talk politics to Picus as speak of the cup with Philip in the room.

"What happened down South?" said Lydia. "London makes me ache for it. I hear the waves turning over—don't interrupt, Phil—and the branches turning round in the wood." Scylla thought: 'Concentrate on Carston. Make him funny—with the fun left out.' Nothing that she said held together, who had Picus and under Gault to tell to the proper person to hear it, *sœur douce amie*. Lydia must know that because of Philip she could not tell. Lydia had refused to dine alone with her. Scylla did not know the stupid scene he had made when Lydia had tried to go, until he had made love to her, and snatched a promise she did not dare break.

Lydia knew and was not consoled. There might be news of Clarence. She was a jealous woman. Scylla had had Clarence to herself: had looked up at Philip, smiling. Already she knew what she had married, what they would become. Soon she would not be with Scylla's people, or even in their world. And Scylla stayed in and walked out of it so airily. Soft, bitter, little laps of far-seeing. The quickest thing to do was hate, before it was taken out of her in sorrow. Hadn't Scylla come to triumph? Her husband's delicious voice and vulgar accent enchanted and fretted her. His words and the beauty of his wrist as he lit Scylla's cigarette. How could she keep him? And keep him Phil? Be sure of him and improve him? Possible or impossible, it was not her job. Who should have been advising Scylla, correcting and fortifying her.

Exasperated, the lion's paw fell, claws astretch.

What follows can be as well represented operatically—it began:

Philip: (recitative) "Lydia and I are often thinking of you, Scylla—and I'm sure you won't take us up wrong."

Lydia: "We were both thinking if it is quite the thing for you to be there alone with all those men!"

Scylla: (song) "Felix is my chaperone, chaperone," etc.

Philip and Lydia: (duet) "In the end it does not do, does not do,

People know you for that kind of woman."

Scylla: "What sort of a woman?"

Philip and Lydia: (recit.) "We feel it since we married. It does not do, it does not do, to go against society."

Philip: "I've seen a good deal of the world, you know—perhaps not quite the same society as yours, but—"

Philip, Lydia and Scylla: (trio) "People say—"

"What do they say?"

"You know the things they say."

"What have they said?"

"We'd rather not tell you and go into details."

"Go into details!"

"You're doing it for MY GOOD."

Philip and Lydia: (duet) "Of course we are, of course we are.

We wouldn't hurt your feelings,

BUT—"

Philip: "I'm so fond of you, Scylla."

Lydia: "We're so fond of you, Scylla.

BUT—

We've found it out, we've found it out.

The world has reason on its side."

Scylla: (solo) "What is the world?

Lydia's world was my world,

And I don't know Philip's world.

What reason has the world got, anyhow?"

Philip and Lydia: (anthem) "IT DOES NOT DO.

IT DOES NOT DO."

Philip and Scylla: (duet) "What good do these men do to you?"

"What good do I do them?"

Philip and Lydia: (quick recitative) "But can't you con-
   sider that every one thinks that you sleep with each
   other in turn?"
Philip, Lydia and Scylla: (trio) "Including my brother?"
   "Now, Scylla, be decent!"
   "I am learning behaviour from you."
   "You're so young,
   So attractive—"
   "I am several years older than you."
Lydia: "You were always a baby."
Philip: "And always the lady."

Philip really said that, and when Scylla giggled, the
string that tied them burned through and snapped. She
remembered Picus at home: under Gault. A cup in a well:
in a house. Out of India: in a book out of no man's land.

> *A shore like that, my dear,*
> *Lies where no man will steer,*
> *No maiden-land.*

Most men steer there, and away before they have properly landed. 'Land me where my friend and her fancy-man
are waiting to bite.' She noticed how they hunted a single
line as a double technique—Lydia wanting to find out,
Philip to defame. It infuriated her that she should be hurt.

Lydia was saying:

"I am awfully fond of those boys, Scylla, but they're *mal
vus.*"

"What is that?" (Don't defend.)

"Well, you know—"

"No, I don't. Try again."

Lydia did:

"Why did you break up so soon? You said Felix had
gone to Paris and you don't seem to know about the others.
Where's Clarence?"

If she knew even that, she would have something to
keep the old heart-break company.

Philip was saying:

"Scylla, why don't you marry Clarence: People say he's a beauty, and it's time you picked up a husband—"

"She wouldn't," said Lydia,—"despises Clarence. But she can't go on like this."

"Go on like WHAT?" Philip answered her.

"You know what people say about a set with no real men in it."

"What is a REAL MAN?"

"They don't amount to anything, and you know it. I've seen the world in my little way, and that sort don't count. I think I've got Lydia out of that kind of thing. We mean to make a good business of things as we find them. Can't finnick about with white hands, old standards, and fancy words these days. Don't mean to, do we? And we shan't get into quite the messes we might find if you asked us down South. Perhaps that's why you don't. And, honestly, I don't know if I'd let Lydia go—"

"If you mean that you'd find Ross having an affair with Nanna, you can go and look."

Philip went on:

"You know we don't mean that. If you'll excuse me, but Lydia said the other day that you're getting to think of nothing but sex—"

Insolent little cub. She had a last look at Lydia, twisting her wedding-ring.

"Of course, I am," she said. "I know something about it. Very naturally, now. I've been trying to tell you. We have all separated now because (not my brother, of course) we can't decide which one of them shall marry me, and we've run away to think; I can't make up my mind. Not Ross, or Picus. But I've decided not to look outside our set."

She saw the blood rising in Lydia's face. Not a blush, a tide to the brain.

'Now I've done it. I've lied. I've hurt her. Considering my present relations with Clarence—'

Lydia was saying:

"I don't know. There is something fatal about your life, Scylla." She noticed that it excited Philip to think of her desired.

A gulf had opened between them, on whose widening edge they shouted brutal farewells. They were telling her that her brother had given dishonoured cheques: that Picus had syphilis: Carston blackmailed: Ross was a satyr and a stunt painter. And Philip that Clarence had shewn cowardice at the front. Then his wife turned on him a look of insanity, and Scylla saw a tiny thread of blood run out of her nostril. A posy stood in Felix's wedding-present, a bowl of flint glass. Philip dashed the water of it on her forehead, and held the sweet scented names to her nose. Lydia struggled up and the bowl was knocked out of his hands and splintered. Scylla had to force herself to laugh, and not to say: 'It's a camp story I told you: invented it, spite for spite.' "I'm going," she said.

Lydia cried: "Is that all that happened?"

Again she almost meant to say 'No, it's a long business. I came here to ask what you thought.' Then was damned if she would.

She said: "What's the good of my staying here? We shall all be back there soon. I'll ask about the syphilis and the satyriasis. Does one put a notice in the papers about Felix's cheques? Shall I tell Clarence to let you know how he escaped court-martial in spite of his seven wounds?"

CARSTON

He was struggling with the branch line of a remote english railway. He got to a place where people changed, and was in the mood to bear with the proceedings of another century.

He had plenty of them before he reached the village called Tambourne. Plenty of fine old women in black-beaded bodices, one button always missing where the strain came over the breasts. Plenty of young live-stock being shifted up and down the line. Plenty of the porters' family party. Plenty of a plate of macaroons locked alone in a glass box in a deserted refreshment room.

Plenty of superb trees, and white nettle-scented dust. At the inn called the Star at Tambourne, plenty of regret for Nanna's fine darned linen and china tea. A night of stars and bats came very slowly. Once out of the wood and away from his relations he asked himself why in Christ's name he had come to see old Mr. Tracy. An ancient of days was living a stroll away from him at Tambourne House. He fetched the cup from his suit-case and put it on the red baize parlour table, a dumb circle of pale green. Why couldn't the thing speak? Just once. Dumb was the word for it. He got rather tight all by himself, but without inspiration. He would have to go and call, have to go call. All up that yellow drive by himself.

LYDIA

She was alone next morning. Philip had gone out to meet a Jew whose favour they were nursing. She had refused, felt she no longer cared if he mismanaged it. She had not spoken since an hour after Scylla had left, and in that hour they had said worse things to each other than they had said to her. But Philip, who had almost cried with fear, in the morning was not dissatisfied. One does not leave the gutter without a few knocks. He had his own plans, his own adventure. Hoped from his heart Scylla was marrying the man. That would get them out of his way for good.

Lydia sat at her writing-table, without her mask, either of love or make-up. Her head, still disfigured, did not belong to this age. She wrote:

> My dear Clarence,
>> How are you all?
> Scylla is up and dined last night. She seemed very well and a little mysterious. I understood, though I may have got it quite wrong, that you're thinking of marrying each other.
>> Please let Phil and me know if it's true. It almost hurts one's feelings not to be the first to wish you luck.
>> No chance of getting away until Phil has pulled off some more business, and then he wants to go to Eastbourne!

She went out herself and posted it to Tollerdown.

Once, down South, one of the boys had called Scylla "bird-alone." They had all asked for names. Picus had been cat-by-himself. Felix, *l'oeuf sur le toit*. Ross, bird-catcher. They had quarrelled a little that morning, and she had not been pleased when Ross had said, grinning: "If Scylla's the bird, one might call you 'wolf-alone'."

FELIX

Felix sobbed in the taxi: "Can't you see we are all damned." And that love and death were one.

They had considerably enlivened the cabaret, a sentimental infamy, its men and girls drunker than the clients. Among their slobbering, rapacious familiarity, the three appeared like drunk young gods. And Felix, a young king receiving his subjects, was courtly to the fawning, swarming band of both sexes in changed clothes. Proud of his companions, unconscious that he was paying for the party, he did not know that Boris owed money there, how he balanced the chance of being dunned with his worth as conductor of a rich client, and hoped that his debt would be put on to Felix's bill. A thing he would not arrange. He had not yet come to that.

Round their table moved the herd of painted animals, Felix's subjects, their tongues parting their lips for what they might get out of the flower-skinned, sapphire-eyed boy, who looked at nothing but Boris. Black briar-rose, he called him, who saw Felix an absurd young splendour. Felix noticed him strange, observant, a moon-baby. Not how the infant was putting two and two together. Nor would he have cared, lifted above any complex of the shopkeeper to be paid in any kind of thanks.

It was the American, later, who developed an intoxicated conscience about Felix when, in the taxi, romantic metaphysics and song gave way to hysteria. He cuffed him roughly into place. Unfortunately, Felix's head broke a window, and all he did was lean out and cry: "I want to suffer as you have suffered, Boris— Police! police!"

The taxi slowed round a corner. He was bleeding from a cut. Boris alone kept his wits. Withdrew Felix's head delicately from the hole in the glass, shouted in Russian at the chauffeur he had picked. Felix had become merely a thing to get home. They pulled up at the Foyot and got him out. Out but not up. The American retrieved the silk hat rolling on the stones: while Boris extracted three hundred francs, taxi, window money and useful change for the next day.

Then came the pilgrimage to which they were hardly equal, in the liftless, ancient barrack, their support to each other physical not moral, an age of social hatred lived through as they hoisted Felix upstairs and round corners, indifferent to his cries that he must *faire pipi*, followed by the concierge jangling the key. Ages of dissimilarity between the American, sudden flower of strength and looks, and the russian-tartar brat of family, to whom neurasthenia had become a habit.

They dumped Felix on the bed. Boris sponged away

the blood, and got off the clothes that would hurt. The blood sickened the other and made him fretful. He gave an odd exhibition of nerves. Boris soothed him and they stumbled downstairs. In the street he said: "I have a little money. Let's go on." The American refused. Boris circled a little on the pavement, and, finding himself alone, drifted off to his little hotel, and slept face-downwards in his only convincing suit.

CLARENCE

At the cottage on Tollerdown, Clarence began a call to order. He had stayed on a night with Ross, the last of them to scatter.

The cottage was indistinguishable from the white, flint-casing chalk rock out of which it was made. God knows when built, its walls sagged in a broken angle with the down-slope. Placed at the mouth of a quarry, he lived naked as could be after his late smothering in trees. A single mountain-ash at the quarry-mouth raised its scarlet against the hot white cutting and the burnt gold grass. From the door a path of glassy flints ran to the cliff's edge, and joined the valley track. At the angle the cliff broke sheer. Four hundred feet below the sea murmured and tumbled on a beach of round yellow stones. Clarence had set the flint path, chipped and cemented them for a touch of construction in an air-haunted land. A place where no sane man would live. But there was generally water in the well-shaft, and just then a blood-mist of poppies on the stony earth, cultivated to just that level. With an ache that he did not understand was for Versailles, Clarence had swung in.

Inside there was not the mess men are expected to make for themselves. A little art and craft, a little cubism, a little chic, made interesting by one of Picus's amusements, models of all sorts of ships.

A viking-boat was a dragon on the sail, a shield-wall along the sides. An Armada-ship, the Virgin all aboard. A lovely proa. A greek galley, and, the first thing Clarence saw, Picus's card at the mast with "A present for Scylla" on it.

Now where did Picus find out how to do them? A family mystery. History did not exist for him. He hated the sea. And that black open boat might have come out of an egg hatched at Salamis.

In the living-room, panelled, and painted a flat jade green, Clarence plumped the scarlet cushions, making everything gay; while in the kitchen, the shepherd's wife set the water running in the cobble channels, skinned rabbits, polished the blue plates. The particular master was back. Long ago, before she'd married the shepherd, and had ten children and lost but three and taken up with the soldiers before he died and his brother had come along, 'twas the same name, and they'd a disease in common, and she'd still be walking over to the camp at Chard, and though she'd lost her teeth, and the better part of her speech, the lads would be over themselves with beer in their pockets, she'd been kitchenmaid at one of the country houses.

She could not read or write, and her time must have been different from ours. Mr. Picus gave her port of an evening, but the one she felt about was Ross. This singular *fille de joie*, over fifty, toothless, palateless, type of disreputable peasant hag, when she knew he was in the land, would stand out on the turf and watch for him. Gobble at Clarence, cooking meticulously the food he would not let her touch: ask if Mr. Ross would be coming over. Scylla terrified her. Nanna laughed at her and was called ma'am.

Clarence strode out, collarless, in riding breeches, to draw water. He looked down into the well, dark fern-ringed tranquillity, round which had happened such a singular little event.

He drew one bucket after another, and sluiced them

over his body, branded with shrapnel and bullet and bayonet thrust.

A vast, delicate strength, not used, not properly understood, piteously alone against the white rock and wash of the blue-wrinkled sea. A scarlet coat in a palace and some gold lace on his shoulders would have fitted him better, watched only as he was by a gasping, furtive old woman behind the kitchen panes. If the other had been there, he would have shewn affectation, talked about his nakedness and her. While Ross and Picus would have skipped through the house and chaffed her if they had noticed her at all. Such was Clarence's audience, with a scattering of poppies, a house huddled against the ground, and below the aphrodite sea.

Indoors he preened and poked everywhere, exceedingly afraid of the coming night. Then he would be alone, the shepherd's wife off at her mincing trudge to her hovel, where occasionally was heard the roar of a carouse. Ross might have joined it and been the life and soul of the party, or lain out sea and star sailing.

Clarence, by himself, was simply and terribly afraid. Not of individuals, but of a menace that walked hand in hand with night, joined with the fear natural in remote places to a man not intuitively tuned. First he told himself that everything would not be ready for Picus, and he would scold him: then that Picus's scenes were a disgrace. Then that Picus was never coming back. Then that it was Scylla who would not let him come back. A rage got him by the throat, shook him, crawled over him. By the time it was night, he was incoherent, and half a dozen times started over the hill to walk seventy miles inland to Tambourne where Picus might be. It was not his humour that checked him, but fear of the vast spaces under the starblazing sky. The stars were not his friends. The Pleiades may have been weeping uselessly for him. When he lifted his eyes up the hills, he averted them. Rough, barrowhaunted places. He shuddered and turned back.

Only candle-light in the cottage, in the silvered sconces on the jade-blue walls. Casket he had made for Picus, hung with brilliant xviiith century paintings of birds. That woman had done it, the slender, cousinly bitch. Once he had thought of dropping the handkerchief at her, and few he'd ever done it to had said no. His extreme vanity had never surmounted the transition from his boy's beauty, which Ross had taken as a matter of course.

'Introvert, introvert' said his mind, full of fashionable fads. Then his torture came on him again as the huge night swept on, and even his fear of it was forgotten in the grinding and tearing of his frustration and desolation and rage against Scylla, until for all human purposes he was mad. In other surroundings it would have been a bad break-down, needing work, praise, new loves, above all admiration. Here, a pebble-throw from a gulf of air, it was ruin for one who in camps and cities and a classic personal relation had been heroic.

The story of the cup, now become a horror, came in. That his reason was not overset was because he took the hollow greek ship with "A present for Scylla" on it, and broke it to splinters.

Next morning he had not slept and sat staring when Lydia's letter came. A horrible fit of laughing frightened the shepherd's wife. She ran home like a half-plucked hen, while Clarence with affected deliberation for some unknown frightful audience took pen and paper and wrote in his exquisite hand.

He told Lydia that it was not so, and in a few lines conveyed such a loathing of Scylla that Lydia half saw the truth, and nearly went to find her. But Philip found the letter amusing, and she did not go.

The levelling afternoon sun that came in through the cottage door found Clarence drawing Scylla, on huge sheets of paper pinned to the walls. In charcoal, obscenely and savagely contorted, and with little darts made of fine nibs and empty cartridge-cases he pierced the bodies of his paper martyrs. Then he tore them down, finding no content in it, so that ragged strips of paper covered the floor, the silver divan, and the cushions bright as fresh blood.

Perhaps he was the man who had suffered most from the disbelief and disuse of all forms of religion. Bred a Catholic, he had left the church and the question superciliously, uneasily. Incapable of Ross's and Scylla's faith that there was a faith, with all its pains and invisibility, unquestioned as air. A religion externalised by a powerful discipline might have upheld him, but all that he had then was a suspicion that this was the punishment of a neglected set of gods.

The hour came when the light began to shew up the earth in relief, with a distinctiveness almost monstrous, like a drug reverie. A little freshness blew in off the water, a cloud or so travelled, teaspoonfuls of fire-dipped cream. Spent with pain, his fear of the night returned.

MR. TRACY

Carston spent the next morning thinking about old Mr. Tracy, or, more exactly, how he would hate to walk up his drive. In his country he would have faced a dozen of them, but he had been out early to scout and had seen the house up a much-too-long-yellow avenue between high clipped shrubs. Unsympathetic. Like a long neck into a trap.

At half-past twelve he had an idea. At two o'clock precisely he had passed the lodge. At two minutes past he saw old Mr. Tracy leave his front door and halt, turning as he walked, to speak to someone within. Two seconds later he saw a neat painted gate in the laurel wall, the entrance of a tunnel. One second later he was mastering the latch, and had disappeared from sight.

We will follow him, as earlier writers say so prettily, as he commences trespasser, in hiding from the approaching master of the house.

He followed the tunnel about ten yards, where it led him on to a wood-path parallel with the drive, whose principal feature was a pavement of enormous roots. He listened to the crisp sound of Mr. Tracy's boots, waited till he had passed, tripped over the roots, slipped down the tunnel again, and reached the house as though nothing had happened. He was ashamed until he noticed that it was a sound instinct that had made him avoid the old man in open.

Half an hour later he was in the library. He heard: "So you want to buy that mischief-making cup for an antiquarian friend in the States? And you want its pedigree? I can write you out the particulars, of course. My name counts for something, but I imagine that I was sufficiently precise last time we met."

"No, sir," said Carston, "you were not. I have its photograph in the book that wasn't burned as thoroughly as you might have wished. There it's described as a mass-vessel, early english, from your collection. Now, I don't give a damn which it is, but it can't be that and a poison-cup. And before I write out a cheque I want to know which."

"But, in any case, Mr. Carston, while we are speaking of money, I imagine that any cheque should be made out to me."

"No, sir. I and three other persons heard you confirm your son's gift of it to Miss Taverner." (His reputation as a collector's at stake. It can't be two things at once)— "As to a second opinion, I expect your British Museum could give us that."

"I admit," said Mr. Tracy, "that it is probably a mass-cup. In my horror of loose feeling I preferred to suggest any origin, however grim or far-fetched, than that my relatives should abandon themselves to superstition."

This might have sounded noble, but Carston kept on. 'Bit of bunk: what has he been up to? That's what I'm not to find out.' He said:

"It seems to me that you've exchanged a fine, mysterious, almost sacred fable for a sordid, even brutal, personal invention. Facts are what I'm here for."

'What I won't get, not the ones that matter.'

"You can be satisfied that in all probability the photograph describes it correctly. An early Church vessel, its shape suggests a chalice, with the setting lost. If so, it might well have been part of a crusader's loot. Incidentally, since its probable origin greatly enhances its value, you might do well to stick to my earlier suggestion, the last part of which is no more than simple fact—"

"Cool!" Carston gasped. Cucumbers and icebergs.

"—Or is to be part of the price for Scylla Taverner's hypothetical virginity?" Carston thought:

'If I start losing my temper, it is he who will find things out. He chose blind-man's bluff. We must play until we needn't.' At the same time conviction came to him that they would find out nothing. His direct attack was obvious, useless, unfruitful.

"I have nothing to say, but that I buy nothing with my eyes shut. And what I've come to get is your reasons for supposing it a Church vessel—" Vain repetition. Not even taken the wind out of the old man's sails. Sailing serenely on: through a weak position: through fraud.

"You shall have them, Mr. Carston, to-night. Signed on my authority. You are staying at the Star?"

IN AND OUT

On his way down the drive Carston knew what you did. In Trollope, in cases of spiritual difficulty, you consulted the vicar. Whether it turned out well depended on whether you found a good vicar or a bad. The landlord directed him. His way led through the churchyard. He noticed a staring white monument, and read on it the name of Picus's mother.

"Old devil to bury her like that and keep it clean." In the flagged hall, he walked up a ribbon of green matting, and saw at the end Picus playing with a blind cord.

"Tracy," he said, "I've been trying to clear this up."

"Any luck?"

"None. Have you a good vicar?"

"I left the churchyard at two in the morning, and said 'It's me,' and I've been here since. Sick of night and mist walking. I've told him. Come in."

* * * * *

Felix woke, rolled over in a flood of gold-spangled dust to find himself lapped in faultless health and spirits. Paris' morning surprise for her children, last night's debauch innocent as a game of kiss-in-the-ring. Last night's resolution clarified and unimpaired. He had Boris to find and explain to him what he had meant. Claim his own. He shaved his hardly perceptible beard, whistling an air from *Louise*. Paris was waiting for him, had given him the day, now in mid-morning, which would only be begun by night.

He ran through his pockets. Boris's address was lost. There were names of unknowns, scrawled on the cabaret cards, not the shred off a bill he remembered, the splendid name scrawled in sucked purple pencil— He rushed out to find his earlier boy friend.

"My dear Felix, how should I know? Those boys sleep anywhere. You might try the quays. You'll see him about again some night."

"I don't mean to wait—I've got to find him, if I go to the police."

"Well, I shouldn't do that— They probably know too much about him." Then, incautiously—"He's probably pretty sick after last night. They say his lungs are going."

Curiously, that fanned Felix. The older boy for the first time liked him well. Wondered if by any chance he saw in his eyes what "one would fain call master." It was odd.

"He used to live somewhere in the nest of hotels round the Rue Buonaparte."

"Good," said Felix. "I'll try them, one by one."

* * * * *

Boris woke up. The young head, a little brutal and afraid in sleep, on waking lost those expressions. "Comme j'ai fait la bombe hier," rubbing his eyes like a baby. A sixth-floor room in a cheap hotel in old Paris has no romantic quality. It was as much as Boris could do to rise nightly like some sort of phoenix out of the ashes of old clothes, torn socks, and russian newspapers. A miserably recognisable room, in a bitter world now burning under the sun-cracked roof, with no room in it for penniless, palace-reared brats. No excuse for the room either. A shameless, shameful pity of disorder, and want not above the trickery. Only on the lavabo shelf there was some sort of order, and a glass full of brushes for the bright white teeth.

What sort of boy was the english boy? Half Boris's nature was curious, the other—it was a nature profoundly divided—had no interest. The indifference lay beneath, the under-waters of the stream that ran in and out, up so many curious creeks, round islands not fixed yet on any map.

His interest was chiefly whether the boy would be good for a few nights of Boris's necessities; some food, unlimited drink, no sympathy, but a kind of companionship. Charm was what he liked, who had it for sole asset. Someone to laugh with. He would have laughed if he could have seen Felix, followed by the taxi he was too impatient to jump in and out of, entering and leaving shabby door after shabby door. He lay on his back and dodged the flies. He was very tired after four years of Paris. Four actual years, but he had never been able to calculate more than a day ahead, which must set ordinary time going differently. Also, what time had he in the sense of future, a bloody curtain between him and his land, his torn roots not fed by the transplanting? Over two hundred francs (the compatriot chauffeur had been merciful) of the english boy's money stuffed away. It might also have startled him had he seen Felix a door nearer, a door further off. One hundred and fifty francs to pacify the old *vache* in the bureau below. If misery had turned the key on him, what of it? Get the second best shoes out of the cobblers. Forget till the money was gone, and in the next spell of rain take cold and go about sore-throated and aching. Till it was time to drink again. Drink to forget. Forget what did not matter. Yet if a fly brushed his caste dignity, he would rage childishly, and laugh and forgive and not forget.

Felix pitched into his room, his heart almost preceding him. Drew himself up and said languidly: "All right after last night?" Poverty that amazed him and he pitied, for a moment dismissing romance for sense.

"Get up and we'll lunch. I'm not in Paris for long. I want you to come away with me."

"Where?" said Boris.

"To my people in England."

"I've always wanted to see England," he said—"we like the english best of all races."

Russians do not gush, and he was arranging his shame about the room; the shirt he had worn last night all he had on him, and his feet grimy and no slippers, and how to turn himself into a desirable object with Felix there; and how to get his clothes out with the bill not paid if he was really going away; and how they couldn't make Felix a cocktail, and would probably refuse to send up so much as a bottle of Vichy; and how soon or if it would be safe to tell Felix about it. And if Felix was really a bore or not. And, suddenly, how bad it was to have to think like that.

And Felix, brimmed with grace, said:

"This was just to tell you. Meet me at the Foyot in an hour."

* * * * *

In another room, in another hotel, in a chaos of elegant poverty, Scylla answered the telephone bell. Philip's voice said:

"What made you let on you were engaged to Clarence the other night? He doesn't seem to think so. Like to hear his letter?"

She was ready for that, through the occasional sense that one has lived through an event before it arrives.

"What's that? I said nothing of the sort. If Lydia likes to think such rubbish. She must have written him one of her letters."

The voice changed:

"I wish you hadn't told her whatever you meant like that. She's been upset."

"Well, she might have married him herself once," and rang off and sat still. This would not do. If their alliance was not to break up, she must get the idea out of Clarence's head. Played into Clarence's hands, she had: to finish her with Picus: give Clarence the game. Subtle-minded, he would know how to bitch things more than they were already bitched. All to bitch Lydia for bitching her. God, what a world! So much for Sanc-Grail cups and maidens. She felt positively superstitious over her own experiences. Then suffered under what seemed, after all, an unfair lack of grace. Then saw the cottage on Tollerdown, a desolation with something in it that raved. Translated it into possibility of annoyance, petty insult, even tragedy. Playing the Freud game, the name rose "Philoctetes." Just the sort of rôle Clarence would pick and play badly. Did Philoctetes play well before he found his Sophocles? Oh! damn analogies. Better go down at once, make at worst an armed peace, and give him something else to think about.

A telegram:

"Arriving shortly with Russian ill to live with us."

Nothing like Felix for letting you know. And Carston had gone to Tambourne with a plan. Picus might be there. Felix was coming back. All roads lay south again. Sleep at Starn that night and go over to Tollerdown in he morning. Have it out with Clarence. Might seduce Clarence and shut his mouth that way. Then to Tambourne and Carston's news.

With serene courage, for she was uneasy, she made her preparations.

* * * * *

Picus introduced Carston to english ecclesiastical life. At last there would be something that he had been led to expect. The old man in his library looked and spoke right.

Picus said:

"I've told him all about it. He's had the devil in his parish."

"Well," said the vicar, "I'll go so far as to say that during the course of our long association, your father has illustrated my picture of hell. And, as usual, any heavenly landscape has been all around and so unobserved." He examined the cup.

"I cannot tell you anything. A piece of worn jade, this time, for the question mark to the question we can none of us answer."

"What is the question?" said Carston.

"Our old friend. Whether a true picture of the real is shewn by our senses alone."

"Can't we leave it that we don't know?"

"Then the picture we have becomes more and more unintelligible."

"I don't know. All I can say is that I've never been so bothered, never behaved so like a skunk, never so nearly fell dead in my tracks till I got down here and began to think about such things. It's unfashionable now, you know—"

"Naturally," said the second old man, so peaceful, so cordially, with such disinterestedness, with such interest. It was going to be a singular ecclesiastic this time. Old Mr. Tracy turned saint. Carston gave up trying to cut providence.

"Can you give us your professional view?" he said.

"My dear man, Picus comes here to be consoled for a grievance because he has given his heart away twice, and doesn't know from which victim to ask it back. You ask my professional advice about this business of the cup; not only for its history, but on the spiritual upsets following its arrival. Here it is: say the seven penitential psalms: go carefully through your failings before man and God: communicate to-morrow at eight: come to matins and sing: attend to my sermon. In the evening sing the Magnificat and remember that when I dismiss you with the prayer *Lighten our Darkness,* I am saying the last word I know. (I suggest a day's devotions because I am sure you have not done any for a long time.) Add to them the lovely sobriety of our church and our liturgy, the splendour of midsummer filtered through old glass on cold stone. That is as far as I can go in my profession, which, like the ancient mysteries, depends largely on what you bring to it. My hope is that some day somebody will bring something. In your case, Mr. Carston, clean hands and a pure heart I'll be bound. I administer formulæ and recall memories—that work and still live. In what lies the scientific triumph but that its formulæ work?"

No one on earth before had told Carston that he had

a pure heart and clean hands. He was startled, touched, nearly cried, and said:

"But we're both in love with Scylla Taverner."

The second old man said:

"Well, I dare say she can do with two fine young men in love with her. She's had no soft life, with her batch of demons."

"He means," said Picus, "that I got off with her and he didn't."

"I hope," said the second old man, "that I'm being asked for my unprofessional opinion."

"We're telling you," said Picus. Carston's courage jumped. He'd been told he had clean hands and a pure heart. Now that it had been pointed out, he saw that it was true.

"Why are you so spiteful about me, Tracy? How do you think you'll get the best out of a man if you fool him, and show you despise him and give your sweetheart away before him?"

"Everyone goes to bed with me," said Picus—"always."

"Now that's a new thing to sulk about," said the vicar. "I am very useless. I cannot tell you about the cup. I cannot judge which of you does or should or could love Picus best. Or Clarence. Or you. His father will probably tell us as much truth as he finds convenient. But when I think of that sensitive, frustrated, pain-racked man who has given his life for you, Picus, alone on Tollerdown, in the fairy-house he made for you—I judge no man. And I do not think it just for you, with your temperament to have the responsibility."

"Nor," said Picus, passionately, "do I."

"Nor," said the second old man, "why Scylla should be your leader and your neglected toy. Nor why you who all wish Felix well should have become his poison. In this business there are no easy answers, and we are left with our honour to lighten us."

Picus said: "Lighten what?"

"This story as I see it," said the second old man, "is true Sanc-Grail. The cup may have been an ash-tray in a Cairo club. But it seems to me that you are having something like a ritual. A find, illumination, doubt, and division, collective and then dispersed. A land enchanted and disenchanted with the rapidity of a cinema. Adventures. *Danger and awe and love.* What has Felix found in Paris that brings him home so quick? Our virtues we keep to serve these emergencies. Our virtue to induce them."

"M'yes," said Picus, —"but there ought to be sharper detail. It was Clarence's spear that started me."

Carston said: "It is true. It has happened like that." He was in a state of consciousness unique to him. Not vision, but wonder become a state, an impregnation of being: that excited and held him in absolute rest. An expectancy more real than the old furniture, the two men with him, the shallow stream that tore past the window, water whistling to itself, a running trap for light.

More than an approach to wonder. Wonder was the answer, and familiar objects out of their categories. He also saw Picus without prejudice, and loved him.

A flock of telegrams was brought in. Carston opened his, brought in from the Star.

"Going to Tollerdown then home come along Felix arriving sick Russian live with us."

"Whoops, my dear," said Picus.

The vicar opened two:

"Coming south take care of us Scylla."

"Is Picus with you? Clarence."

"The grail knights are gathering, it seems. This only I see clearly. Either this is a curiously coincidental hash, or we are taking part in events, only part of which are happening on the earth we see. Meanwhile, I approve the spacious dust-bin into which you throw most things, and have seen everything thrown."

"Then you believe there is a moral search?" said Carston, ignoring what paralleled with his wonder.

"I do. Even unprofessionally. As valid and as open to revision as research in the electromagnetic field. Practically I advise you to stick to your tastes as gentlemen and your love of art. You're so damnably proud and fastidious you'll do that anyhow."

"Felix," said Carston, eloquently, "I really couldn't do justice to the way that boy behaved. The way he treated his sister; has and will again."

"He seems to be arriving from Paris on an orgy of tending the sick."

"Feeding the hungry," said Picus. "I know Russians. I wonder what we're in for?"

The second old man said:

"I'll take him off your hands if he is any good. The young are getting worth watching again."

Carston said:

"I wish the cup could be disposed of."

"I'll go over to the Star," said Picus, "and wait for my father's idea of convincing you. I've a lech on the boots."

When they were alone, Carston said with an effort:

"My intentions are very sincere towards Scylla Taverner."

"I think they are. So are his. I'll marry her to either of you with a psalm of joy if it works out that way. But you do realise that your relation with her will not be the same as hers with Picus? Young men think sex is all the same, or at best a sacred or profane love, when it's as varied as art."

They chatted. Picus brought back a letter with a black seal.

Cup found in the vestry in the church of St. Hilary-under-Llyn sometime in July 1881. Given me by the rector, the rev. John Norris, as it could not be identified as church property. Believed by me, on the authority of (a string of names followed), *to be a cup of the rare but occasionally found chalices of the Keltic church.*

"The Llyn is on the Welsh marches," said the vicar, "and the man's dead."

Carston said:

"Then we get nowhere."

"Nowhere. Only in ghost-stories, and those not the best, do you get anywhere that way."

"But what are we going to do with the damned thing? It can't lie about the house like a green eye that doesn't wink. The man's dead. Suppose the authorities stick by Mr. Tracy. Or don't? This has been a fool's errand—"

"I have an idea," said the vicar. "Take it back to Tollerdown and replace it where you found it. If the next drought sends it up in a suspicious manner, well and good. It seems to like wells. And truth, if she prefers not to talk, can return to one."

Carston said: "I like that."

"Good," said Picus, "learn it to be a toad." Both prayed he would add—"I'll be off with it and look up Clarence."

Not at all.

"I'm not ready yet. Someone had better take it and fetch him. And Scylla. He gets ideas in his head when he's alone there. Carston, you started travelling about with the thing. Go and drop it and bring them back. There's a train to-morrow that starts at six."

CLARENCE and SCYLLA

Scylla slept at Starn. She overslept. A terrific heat had sprung up, and made her feel that there was danger in approaching the hills.

Neither Ross nor Clarence had been seen at Starn, only Nanna had driven in on the baker's cart to conduct her favourite campaign about the quality of preserving sugar.

"She just wouldn't listen to me, ma'am. All she 'ud say was that she wouldn't have you or your raspberries poisoned by what I'd sent." The grocer's wife told her.

So Nanna was making jam. Felix was partial, especially to raspberry jam. Russians put it in their tea. It was after lunch that she discovered that there was not a car to be had, and also took a lift off the baker down the valley to Tollerdown. She bumped and swayed over the flint-dressed road, the white dust powdering her, the overwhelming sun bearing her down, until the driver pulled up at the valley's end, an earshot from the sea, under the hill.

Vast its burnt gold desert shoulder rose beside her, the ribbon path bleached and crumbling. She went up. Struggle with fire and earth and steepness upset her physically: her arms were red, her neck beaded with sweat, her chemise stuck to her skin. Poor nymphs of Artemis. What complexion could stand it? That was why they were painted hunting in woods. Half-way up she sank on a stone and fanned herself with her hat. Remembered another walk, to Starn. She feared that Clarence had seen her, was sulking inside instead of coming to meet her. That was sad. She remembered how once in London she had come to him straight back from Spain, and he had lifted her up and carried her over the threshold, so glad he had been to see her.

Clarence had not seen her. Unshaved, half-dressed, he was trying to torture the body of Picus, the statue he had done of him in clay. He had dragged it out against the quarry wall and pierced it with arrows of sharpened wood, feathered from a gull he had shot overnight.

Scylla found the door open and went softly in.

"Clarence, I've come all this way. Can I have tea?"

He heard the low voice, thought of the gull crying. She saw the bird's half-plucked body, bloody on the floor, and that there were papers torn in strips and little darts. She turned over a fold and saw her own body, and her cry was more like the gull. Bird-alone in the lonely room. Except for a ghost called Clarence, everything was empty. She thought:

'Run away: Can't: Where to? It's all empty, and my

knees shake. And I'm curious. Curious and furious and only my body is afraid.'

Clarence wanted to be sure about the bird. He came in slowly, dazed with violence and grief. Bad conscience and fear of making a fool of himself nagged his blazing obsession. He saw Scylla at the door in silhouette, her scarf fluttering off the back of her neck, sweat-darkened curls appliquéd on her forehead, her hat thrown familiarly on a chair, her mouth open.

"Come and look," he said, and with the fingers of one hand dug into her collar-bone, led her through the kitchen into the half-circle of quarry behind.

She saw Picus in greenish clay, pricked with white feathers. Clarence had made him exactly as he was, a body she had known, for which hers ached.

"You see," he said, "I only had what I'd made of him to do it to."

There was an arrow through his throat, and his head had not fallen forward.

"You're going down the well, where the cup came—"

"Why, Clarence?"

"Best place for you, my fancy-girl. If there's enough water, you'll drown. If there isn't, and I don't think there is, you'll break every bone in your body."

She could run like a lapwing, but he could run fast. She was strong as a tree-cat, but he could tear her in two.

"I came to bring you to Picus. He does not want you to be alone on Tollerdown. He is at Tambourne. Lydia sent you a silly letter because" (get his vanity if you can) "she is so in love with you that she's mad."

"And so are you, it seems. Gods! I'm a lucky chap. Unfortunately, Picus doesn't join the harem. He doesn't like me any more.

"Going to marry me, are you? You shall in a way. I mean to follow you down the well."

"Picus is at Tambourne, waiting for you."

"In time he will be here again. My body will fetch him."

"You are the most beautiful man in the world, but you won't be when they get you up out of the well."

He took her other shoulder in his fingers, thrusting them into the muscle-hollow under her neck, hurting her. She forgot him exacting, petulant; remembered him long before, beautiful, merry, inventive, good. And cruel now. Stupid cruelty. Cruelty frightened her. She lied:

"Clarence, I am going to marry Carston—I teased Lydia—" He turned her towards the well.

"There will be one less of you bitches to come into our lives."

"We bear you, and I am no stronger in your hands than that bird. Why did you shoot a gull? It isn't done." Time seemed very precious. Only a thimbleful left. The well very near. The sun turning a little away from them.

"Woodpecker," she shrieked, and flung Clarence off, and ran to the statue. She had been so careful not to say that name, and now saw Clarence hurrying to her, the mournful crazy mask splitting, the mouth turning up, the eyes shooting death at her. And Picus, pierced with arrows, smiled down his sweet equivocation. She heard: "That'll do better." He had a cord round his waist. He had cattle-ranched once: that was his lariat. She ran once round the statue. A second later he had thrown her, picked her up half-stunned and tied her against Picus. A black flint had cut her head, a patch of blood began to soak through the moon-fair hair.

Clarence walked back and stood by the kitchen door, fitting an arrow to the string. It ripped the skin on her shoulder and entered the clay. She saw another fly towards her and notch her forearm. Another, and there was a tearing pain below her left breast.

Three instants of pain, set in one of fear. Like a great jewel. Clarence stood by the kitchen door, sharpening an indifferent arrow. She made a supreme effort: not to scream much: not to betray herself. Then a moment of absolute contempt of Clarence. Then of pain. Then, as if she were looking out of a window, into a state, a *clarté* the other side of forgiveness. Not by that route. She fainted.

CARSTON and CLARENCE

Carston's day had been a penance. A train had landed him some time in mid-morning at a place called Chard. Picus had said that it was nearer Tollerdown than Starn, but no one there had heard of the place. The station lay in no immediate relation to the village. The inn was fusty and unsympathetic. The heat atrocious. A day for no sane man to tramp while the sun was high. Miles across another bend of the heath where Picus had lost him, the down-banks rose, aery turf walls, solid as flesh and blood. One of them was Tollerdown. He held up a passing motorist, who was kind. He gave him a lift down a white road sprung like an arrow across the moor that filled the lowlands like a dark dragon's wing.

At the foot of the turf, he set Carston down. "Go up the track," he said, "and make towards the sea. If it's not this shoulder, it's the one that follows it." Carston mounted, into silence, on to height. He had never been so well in his life, could not have stood that if he had not been so well. Never had his heart been so touched. Could he stand that?

He mounted, past the trees, the copses, the gorse patches, on to the last crest of raw grass. The earth and the sea extended in a perfect circle round him. He had only to follow the hill's spine, and drop half-way into the valley to strike the cottage before he walked over into the sea. Like a man who has been given a heavy treasure that he has not looked at and must carry home, he walked on.

Bear your burden in the heat of the day, he sang, who had been in great request at parties for his bawdy repertory.

His track ran through five barrows. By one was a crook-backed angry thorn. A bad patch. He passed it, glad to have left them behind, keeping his face towards the sea. Interlude this day alone, in a train. On a hill. Find a cottage on a shelf. Console its inhabitant. Bring him a cup to pop down a well. Fetch him away. You could make a ballad about it. About a mile more to go. *One more river to cross.* The turf turned over in what was almost a cliff. He was not on Tollerdown. Picus and the man in the car had said two hills. This one dropped into a narrow neck. The great bank he could now see rising on the other side, that was Tollerdown. He cursed, slid down the break-neck path, over a wall of unmortared stone bound with bramble that ripped his clothes; across a field, ploughed and deserted, its furrows baked to iron. Over a gate crested with barbed wire, whose rusty thorns drew blood from his knee. Sprinted down a sparkling grit road, met cattle and an angry dog. Hurry, hurry, he did not know why. Get this over. Hanging about an eternity he'd been, up in the air. Now for people and the end of the cup. A baker's cart passed him on the road, directed him, and he found himself mounting again by the way Scylla had come. Stopped at the open cottage door, knocked, waited, went in. He saw the bird. The torn papers. He went through.

He saw Clarence, slowly and awkwardly trying to re-string the bow, and the lovely nightmare, Scylla hanging bound to the stake of her love. His reason had vanished. Returned, abnormally clear. A madman and the girl probably dead. No gun. Behind them a gulf to the sea. Was I made a man for this? *Lighten our darkness.*

Play-act. He pulled out the cup. It had kept its jade-coolness. He shewed it to Clarence.

"Just got here. Picus wants it put back in the well, and you to come to Tambourne. See? Sent me." He took his arm: "Put it in yourself. He said you were to. Drop it in. Feel how cool it is. Wants to get back to where it came—into water. He'll be wretched if you don't."

Clarence staggered a little, moving towards the well.

"My head's not cool," he said. "Hurts like hell. The boy wants it dropped in. I can't see why I should attend to all his fancies."

Carston tried not to look at Scylla, not let him turn. Clarence's step shambled a little, his head dropped.

"I'm not to do it. Only you."

"All right. Here goes." Plop went a noise a very long way below them. Clarence covered his eyes with his hands.

"Dear man, it was decent of you to come. Such a way and the country strange to you. Hope you had a car. D'you mind if I go in for a bit and fix you up some tea?" Carston guided him carefully, back turned from what was out there in the sun, into the house-shadow, into the studio.

"I'll make tea. You lie down a bit." He was thinking how to lock him in, when the young man dropped, moaning that his head hurt, and that something was trying to get out through his eyes. Carston hoped it might be the tears he'd cry when he knew what he'd done. He had always liked Clarence, disliked that his affection should have turned to horror. He even put a cushion under his head. Then snatched up a knife in the kitchen, rushed out and cut Scylla free, and carried her on to the sitting-room couch. Then followed a time when time indefinitely suspended and extended itself. Attempts to withdraw the wood that pierced her, to stop the blood, to revive her, sustain her, dreading her consciousness and her unconsciousness alike. Listen to Clarence moaning, listen for him moving. He had not found a key to lock him in. Try to find a revolver without leaving Scylla, and later not to fall over the gun he had laid across the table at full cock. At one time he wondered if he should pitch Clarence over the cliff while he went for a doctor, and went nearly mad as the light failed, for he saw her coming back to her right mind alone, and the ghost of the man who had injured her crawling up the cliff-face to go on with his dream out of the flesh, and two ghosts, not one, would carry on, the torturing and the tortured.

* * * * *

An immensely long shadow flung back was travelling the hills. As the sun slipped incandescent into a crescent of far cliff, Carston heard outside whistling, liquid notes of everything that has wings. He remembered, 'Like Mozart.' Thought it might be death, coming sweetly for Scylla, as Picus walked into the house.

He saw Carston glaring, feeling for the gun, heard him say:

"You sent her to this. You laid this trap for her. You drove him mad—"

He answered:

"If that were so, should I have sent you? Should I have come myself? Whisht man, let's look." Passing, he put the gun at safe, and Carston saw him lay Scylla's body across his knees, open the chemise he had slit up and re-tied with a scarf.

"Scylla, you silly bitch, wake up. Man, I know all about wounds. Side glanced off a rib, the rest's nothing."

"All but our cruelty to her. I've not been that."

"No, you've not. Less than us. Yes, call it my fault. I can be sane. Where's Clarence?"

"In the studio, not quite conscious. I can't find the key."

"He'll do. Scylla's quite comfy here. Go and make her some tea. Stiff whisky for us. Clarence had a bad head wound. With that and the sun, and my bitchery— Where's the cup?"

"In the well. I made him put it down. Said it was your orders. Then he collapsed."

"Where did this happen?"

"At the back. Go and look."

Picus went out into the quarry and looked at the statue of himself. Spots of Scylla's blood, blackening in the dying light. None of his own. He took an axe from the woodpile and knocked the image of himself to a stump. Carston heard the dry pieces falling, the patter of dust.

* * * * *

Scylla stirred and sat up. Two cups of tea pressed to her lips met and clicked together.

"I can't drink out of two cups at once." Carston withdrew his. She drank.

"Is it Picus?" she said, feeling for their hands.

Carston said:

"Is there nowhere in this hell-forsaken country where we can get a doctor?"

"She doesn't need one," said Picus—"only us. No, love, I won't go away. We're going to sleep here. Hush, love. I've got to do magic and make you well. Better magic than at Gault."

"What's happened to Clarence?"

"We've put him in the studio. His head's all wrong. To-morrow he won't remember about this."

"He isn't coming back? Picus, I don't know how. Lydia wrote an idiot letter. I just came in. Not to be beastly, but to try—" She began to cry a great deal. Carston stayed with her. Picus went to the studio alone.

Soon he came back with an armful of bedding. He laid it on the floor.

"He's asleep. He will sleep."

"What are we going to do?" cried Carston, at exhaustion's breaking point.

"Sleep. We shall all sleep. Where we are, round her. Cover her over. Put a drink for her in the night. Finish the whisky. So. We shall all sleep. You at the foot. I at the side. On this side, love, or you'll lie on the cut in your hair.

"Shoes off, Carston. We shall need our feet to-morrow.

"Door open, and perhaps a rabbit will come in.

"Sleep, man, sleep. We must. Scylla, that's a fat star winking. Clarence is locked in. Had a turn like this before, and thought he was a nun."

Carston heard a giggle.

Of course, if Picus said a rabbit would come in. If Scylla wanted a rabbit to come in. . . .

* * * * *

The shepherd's wife sat up on a heap of rag quilts. The thatch bore down over a window sunk in the rubble wall, the panes wood-squared, double-fastened with paint, the ledge filled by a tropical green geranium, flowerless, filtering the light. The shepherd snored.

"Get up!" she squealed, and kicked him. "I be going across to the house."

A little later the old trollop left the rustic slum, and was crossing the hill's dewy shoulder in the delicate light. The day before she had been afraid to go; but in the night, encouraged by a bottle of whisky, she had seen Mr. Ross in a dream.

Clarence had built the studio out into the quarry at the back. She looked in first at its window and saw him sleeping there. Always out and about early he was. Picus had left the key outside in the lock. She went in. Clarence woke. There was a pain in his brain that felt like a nut. Before there had been a worm in the nut, but that had gone to sleep. He had felt the nut before. In a day or so there would not even be a nut, certainly not what went before the nut, the worm boring and making a wild pain that made a wild dream, on the edge of whose memory he was living.

"You're early," he said—"Get some tea." And I'm in my clothes. "And mind you put it in with the teaspoon."

He went to the well to sluice himself and saw his statue in bits. Looked up for a rock-fall from the quarry, which was impossible. Found bits of wood and feathers sticking in the clay and strode back to the kitchen. Heard her clacking that indeed she didn't know, and that the living-room door was locked.

He went round to the front, to the open door, saw where a hare had made her form. Looked in and saw, still sleeping, Picus, Carston, Scylla. He shook his friend's shoulder gently:

"Hi, boy, what's happened?" Picus woke at a touch, pointed outside and rose silently.

"Who's taken my statue outside and smashed it?"

"Come out with me. Out and down a bit. A boat's in. Down at the Lobster Pot they'll fry us fish."

"But I'm not shaved. Can Carston fix up some breakfast for Scylla? Does he know the old woman can't? What's happened, lad? You look like a wet Sunday. Headache again?"

"No. Only you must come on."

He dropped sharply down the hill, Clarence behind him. He felt his mouth twist into a sneer. Clarence the kindly host, the country-gentleman making the best of a cottage and lack of retainers. Then that contempt was unjust. The unfamiliar concept of justice and injustice stuck and was accepted.

Then that punishment was on him. He had to operate on Clarence, not prick and bewilder. Had to undo his arts, his graces, his wit. Clarence's first protection would be to turn on him. A man of perverse and subtle mind, he would be quick to distort to save himself. Making me think.

Then at the Lobster Pot he acquired immediately tea, butter, bread, jam, and the first batch of the landlady's personal fish.

"Damned hungry," said Clarence, helping him to the one small real sole.

Ouf. Why did Clarence look so lovingly at him, when for the first time on record he threw it back on to his plate?

He did not like being hurt. The others were more used to being hurt. Now that he had to hurt, he did not want to. (A reaction impossible to Carston, for whose race sadism is not fun but a serious expression.)

Ow. How much he cared for Clarence, for sport and adventure and work shared. More than them all. Except Scylla. Because that love was shot through with something like an arrow and the feather of a bird. The blood on her white shoulder, the rose feet and feather of a bird.

Ai. His breath came on different sighs. *One more river to cross.* To be sure that he did not act, in this, in any way like his father. That understood, he left his desperate network of light and dark and gave himself up: neither to Clarence, nor to fear: but to a space full of clear forms and veritable issues. What he must do in order not to be any way like his father. Was that to give himself to Scylla? He had met her on his path. So. The bird's thought darted into a song:

> *So every way the wind blows this sweetie goes in the South.*

While Clarence saw an assurance like maturity drawing itself in the set of the head and the subtle mouth.

Picus looked for a moment out to sea, and began:

"What have you been doing the last three days, since I went off to Tambourne?"

"Stayed on with Ross a bit. Walked over. Got the place shined up."

"It must have been pretty hot?"

"The sun bored like worms into your head."

"What happened then?"

"There was lots to do, but I found the nights, short as they are, damned long. When it isn't dark and it's going to get dark and you listen out. You know. But in places like this you can never tell what day which happened."

"What was yesterday like?"

Clarence screwed round, ever so little equivocally.

"I sort of remember that something rather miserable happened in the morning. Might have been a letter." And quickly—"But I can't account at all for the statue being in bits. I know you'll say it doesn't matter what happens to my work, but Ross liked it. You said you liked it yourself—"

"Looksey," said Picus, tenderly—"you've got to know, you know. You went off the deep-end again."

"You mean I smashed it myself?"

"No. I did a bit. I mean I broke it. I felt I had to."

Clarence listened gravely, his eyes still altering their angle.

"Well, if you thought it bad, that's that. But you've taken so much of my life, do you think you should do in my work, also?"

"It wasn't for that. You've forgotten about yesterday. You said something miserable happened, and it did." (Now are his eyes shifting memory or madness?) "Remember when you thought you were a nun? This time you must have thought you were Apollo, or a roman official with an early christian. There was some story in town, and Lydia sent you a letter. And Scylla came down here on purpose to clear it up and fetch you along. She found you shooting at me, and you tied her up and shot her. Carston came over and probably saved her life. I followed, and by then you'd got through your fit and were asleep. She isn't badly hurt. That's what happened. Why I brought you down here. And you can kick me for my fantasies and tempers. Half the blame's on me." Is this going to release me? Have I been looking for that? *This sweetie goes?*

"It's another of your stories," Clarence said.

"Go up and see."

"Excuse to put me in an asylum. I get you."

"Balls, man. The old man at Tambourne, the vicar, I mean c'd explain. Tell us what we could do."

"His orders aren't even valid."

"Don't know what you mean. Go and see. You tied her

with the lariat. You shot a gull to wing your arrows. There's one struck her shoulder and her side. After Carston had cut her down, I smashed myself up with the axe. Sort of apology."

"Did I really shoot a gull?"

"You shot her till she fainted."

"Did I drag your statue out and shoot you?"

"Picked me out carefully."

"It was the best thing I've done, but I haven't hurt you, boy?"

"You threw Scylla. She cut her head on a stone. Carston took an arrow out below her left breast. She was pinned to me by her shoulder—"

"Getting kick out of it, aren't you?"

"Go and see."

"And face that dumb fool Carston."

"Look at Scylla."

"Where's the cup?"

"You put it in the well."

Silence, while Picus watched the bright, brown close-set eyes turn this way and that. Never into his eyes. Never out to sea. Over his shoulder, at the fish-bones, into his cup.

"It's a clever way of breaking things up. You say that you came later?"

"An hour. You were lying in the studio. You were saying something about worms and time and cups. I think you know, that you actually *did* a dream."

His simplicity amazed Clarence: made him thoughtful.

"I am sure that you're letting Carston take you in. You're simple sometimes, bless you. You weren't there. He found me a bit off my head and I went in and fell asleep. As a matter of fact, I don't remember yesterday.

"I'm going up. You might stay and see if that net we broke is mended and follow. I even think you believe this, but it is more likely to be some revenge of Carston's—"

It was suggested to him, fretfully and quite unjustly,

that Carston could neither improvise a bow and arrows, throw a leaded cord, or hit a sitting haystack. And it was painful on their present undertaking to see Clarence stride off to clear up the affair. Picus fidgeted about the beach and threw unsuccessful ducks and drakes. One suddenly skimmed out. So much for that.

And every way the wind blows this sweetie goes in the South.

* * * * *

Clarence followed him full of anger, full of breakfast up the hill. Then, as he climbed and felt the strengthening sun, of a kind of catchy fear. The nut was shrinking. How was he to persuade Carston that they had not been entertained by a sadist? The business faintly excited him. With each step he felt the sun's menace. He wanted to be alone under the cool thatch and whittle at a mazer he was making to hold punch at parties. A present for Scylla.

The night before Carston had thrown out the half-plucked gull over the cliff. It had caught on a bush, and almost at the door Clarence saw the torn white rags. He stood a long time while the dew dried.

"I suppose I thought she was the bird." The whole memory came back. The nut in his head dissolved like a drop of wax. His skull filled with pure memory.

The figure he had cut with his excuses. How save his reputation for sanity? With Picus. With all of them?

What does one do when one has done a thing like that?

How act a repentance unfelt as yet, only betrayal by time, chance, magic, interfering friends, offending gods?

The gull, held on a twig by a pinion-feather, loosened, balanced a second, and vanished over the cliff.

"I must follow," he said, "now."

The sun had thrown his shadow to the threshold. Carston saw it and said nothing, afraid, helping Scylla to splash in water smoky with most of her host's scents, combing the blood out of her hair. Sweet to have her safe and look after her. Then he heard her say, "There's Clarence." She had seen him at the cliff's edge. Carston held that he waited to be seen, but in truth he had forgotten Carston and Scylla. Carefully looking not down but out to sea. Taking a last pull at memories there.

Of Picus. Of the band he had grown up with. Of war, whose issues he had found too simple. Of their spiritual adventure he had not been equal to. Of the fool he had made of himself. The revenge his death would be. Not stay to be called Judas. *And bring our souls to His high city.*

He took a step to the edge. Scylla jumped off the divan, and with her hand at her side, ran out to him.

"Clarence, come in."

She had hold of him as he had held her.

"What'r'you doing out in your chemise?"

"You know. Come in."

"Get me," she said to Carston, "a wooden bowl in the studio, and a green baize roll of tools." She lay down again. Clarence paced about once or twice, and sat down beside her.

"There's going to be an awful party over at the house. Felix is bringing home a Russian."

He said:

"I'm not mad. No need to go on like that. I remember. The bird made me."

"Did you think I was it?"

"No. There was a letter, and the sun and you know my head."

Look," she said, and pulled off the handkerchief that tied her shoulder—"and my head is cut and my side. It was partly my fault that Lydia wrote to you. Go on carving while we talk."

He did as she told him. Carston watched them. Like an idyll: a young lover making a present for his sweetheart, sitting on her bed. A harrow of wild geese with their necks out at flight. A border of fish.

"It ought to be set. Can you work in silver, Clarence? We might melt down that atrocious salver—"

Insufferable to be hushed like this. He preferred Carston glaring at him, wondering if he should get the gun. Picus came in.

"D'you know now?"

"Yes. And I'm not fool enough to imagine that there's any apology or excuse. Or forgiveness that isn't from duty or impulse. You can have Scylla."

"I knew you'd take it wrong," said Picus. "We're not talking about beds and we know who we'll sleep with. What you ought to know is—"

"Look here," said Carston. "You've had a touch of the sun. We'll grant that. Scylla has a fool female friend in London, fool enough to be in love with you. Wrote you a spiteful letter you lap up. Scylla comes down to explain it and comfort your feelings, and you try to kill her by torture. I know you were mad. If you don't pull yourself together and try and face it, everyone will know you were mad; for you'll do it again outside your home circle. The world won't make delicate excuses for you, you spoilt, hysterical, self-pitying, self-centred, uninventive, incompetent son of a bitch."

"Not uninventive," said Scylla, "but you'd better try something else."

"I'm taking you over to Tambourne right away. We'll start now, and you can wait at the inn while I get a car. The old parson there is the company you need. You can come back to Gault, if they want you, when you've got your senses back."

Picus nodded. "We are all for you, Carston."

"All of us," said Scylla.

"Don't say," he answered, "That if I stay here much

longer, I shall be one of you. Because I never shall, and I don't want to be."

"Our house is your house," said Scylla.

"Besides," said Picus, "did you ever enjoy a summer more?"

"Hasn't it been better than a movie? Leave Clarence at Tambourne and come over and look at Felix's find."

In his heart he knew he would not. Though there was continuity in this adventure, a circle like the design on Clarence's mazer, a ring near to a magic ring, he knew that nothing would induce him to go back to that poverty and pride, cant and candour, raw flesh and velvet; into that dateless, shiftless, shifting, stable and unstable Heartbreak House. Not for a bit. Off to Paris on his own folkadventure. In his last moments with them, looking at Clarence's bowl, he saw the changes in things.

There had been an apple once. There had been an apple tree. When it gave no more apples, it had made fire, and a slice of its trunk had become a bowl cut out into birds. The bowl unless it was turned into fire again, would stop growing and last for ever. Things that came out of time, and were stopped; could be made over into another sort of time.

Clarence sat silent, a tear or so falling, shame and anger mounting. Once away, he would leave Carston; would not go to Tambourne. He would go to Tambourne because he must have somewhere to hide. The old parson might have comfort for him while Picus was with Scylla, and she enjoyed the reward of warriors. She and Picus alone together, playing at happy warriors.

If there was nothing for him at Tambourne, there would still be Picus's father, a fine story to pick over together.

He said:

"Perhaps you'll send my clothes. We must go before

mid-day. I shouldn't like Carston to have a repetition before he gets me to Tambourne."

And bring our souls to His high city.

He took Scylla's hand, remained a moment in her embrace. Carston followed him down the hill.

* * * * *

That afternoon cloud flecks flew over and the wind freshened. Ross and Nanna left the house scented with boiling sugar and took a walk down to the sea. He listened to a comparative history of her jam-making and a sketch of her intentions about the vegetable marrows with the interest he gave to each man on his subject alike. From the cliff above the fisherman's hut they saw a ketch running before the south wind, straight for the bay.

"A french boat," he said, "they're running her in too close to the reef." The old nurse shaded her eyes.

"It's Mr. Felix steering. In a hurry he is as usual. It's a nice way to bring his friend home." Silence. A Russian brought over in a fishing-smack: in a hurry. The ketch made the channel (where the bluff hid it from the coastguards' telescopes and the sooner the better), and Ross saw Felix and a sailor drop into a dinghy and pull fast for shore. In the stern sat another. They went down to the water's edge to meet them. A few strokes out, Felix sprang thigh deep in the weed and dragged up the boat till her keel scraped the rocks. He embraced Ross, turned and gave the boy a hand to spring to shore.

"Ross, this is Boris."

"But what made you come this way?"

He thought that he was looking at something at the same time old and young. A youth he understood. An age he did not. Also that it was worn and tired and sick. And that Felix's eyes were like dark-blue coals, his step certain, his voice without petulance.

"I had no papers," said Boris.

"We got into a row," said Felix, "the police raided a café, and we did a bolt. We ran straight into two men up a back street and sent them spinning. One was hurt. Then I saw that it was no good, especially for Boris, and got a car to the coast. Paid up those chaps to bring us and cut back. There's a third man below to replace Boris in case we were seen from the shore."

Not bad for Felix. Ross looked again at what he had brought, standing on the tide-mark, his back to the water, the ooze soaking his poor shoes. The sailors landed two suit-cases.

"See here," he said, "and excuse us. D'you mean you have no papers and no papers you can show—?"

"He's a White," cried Felix, "and he lost them."

Boris said: "That is exactly so."

"And you're not running dope, or away from any crime worth mentioning?"

"On my honour, no— I need a holiday and your cousin was good enough—"

Ross saw that, so far as it went, this was true. The vistas opening were more oblique. He had only to look at that head in its sea-wide aureole, the high forehead and temple-thinned black hair, the slanted cheekbones, and observant green eyes. From the remote east. Out of the sea. Lovely, ugly, helpless, high-born thing. Whipcord and ice and worn out. Wangle him papers in London.

"Boris, our stranger," he said. "Our nurse."

Boris kissed her hand. They climbed the little cliff path. At the top he began to look around him.

Out at sea, it had been land, earth under his feet after a night and day's pitching. Land: an interesting new place. Another people who might have no use for him. Why should they? No longer in doubt, soon there would be food and a bath and fresh linen and bed, he took a look at England. He saw a line of treeless hills, a puzzle of fields; under his feet a pattern of sweet herbs. An arrow of wood they entered, into a tunnel of light where birds broke cover, green even under the feet. A house where the windows were doors and stood open, in front of which a yucca, taller than a man, had opened its single flowerspike. Over the house, a hill turned wall. Into a room where air and bees whispered, honey smelt and the sea. And something he remembered: the smell of fruit bubbling in copper pans, in a kitchen—a child with his nurse—in a country-house, in Russia, in a pine forest.